RECOGNIZE!

RECOGNIZE!

AN ANTHOLOGY HONORING AND AMPLIFYING BLACK LIFE

Edited by

WADE HUDSON

and

CHERYL WILLIS HUDSON

Crown Books for Young Readers

New York

Compilation copyright © 2021 by Just Us Books, Inc.
Jacket art copyright © 2021 by Floyd Cooper
Front flap art copyright © 2021 by James E. Ransome

All rights reserved. Published in the United States by Crown Books for Young Readers, an imprint of Random House Children's Books, a division of Penguin Random House LLC, New York.

Crown and the colophon are registered trademarks of Penguin Random House LLC.

Photograph and contributor credits begin on page 183.

Visit us on the Web! rhcbooks.com

Educators and librarians, for a variety of teaching tools, visit us at RHTeachersLibrarians.com

Library of Congress Cataloging-in-Publication Data
Names: Hudson, Wade, editor. | Hudson, Cheryl Willis, editor.
Title: Recognize! : an anthology honoring and amplifying Black life /edited by Wade Hudson and Cheryl Willis Hudson.
Description: First edition. | New York: Crown Books for Young Readers, [2021] | Includes bibliographical references. | Audience: Ages 10+. | Audience: Grades 4–6. | Summary: "An anthology featuring over thirty Black authors and illustrators to honor Black life past, present, and future"—Provided by publisher.
Identifiers: LCCN 2021022586 (print) | LCCN 2021022587 (ebook) | ISBN 978-0-593-38159-5 (hardcover) | ISBN 978-0-593-38160-1 (library binding) | ISBN 978-0-593-38161-8 (ebook)
Subjects: LCSH: African Americans—Literary collections. | American literature—African American authors. | Children's literature, American. | CYAC: African Americans—Literary collections. | American literature—African American authors—Collections.
Classification: LCC PZ5 .R235 2021 (print) | LCC PZ5 (ebook) | DDC [Fic]—dc23

The text of this book is set in 12-point Century Monotype.
Interior design by Trish Parcell
Hand lettering by Adrian Meadows and Sylvia Bi

Printed in the United States of America
10 9 8 7 6 5 4 3 2 1
First Edition

To Bernette G. Ford, our friend and comrade in children's book publishing. A true trailblazer who for decades advocated for diversity and inclusion in the publishing industry, her legacy will continue to inspire across generations.

To all those who know and have always known Black life matters, and to Nikki Grimes, who suggested this anthology, which gives testimony to it.

CONTENTS

"It's important for us to also understand that the phrase 'Black Lives Matter' simply refers to the notion that there's a specific vulnerability for African Americans that needs to be addressed. It's not meant to suggest that other lives don't matter. It's to suggest that other folks aren't experiencing this particular vulnerability."

—PRESIDENT BARACK OBAMA

FOREWORD

"No one is born hating another person because of the color of his skin, or his background, or his religion. People must learn to hate, and if they can learn to hate, they can be taught to love, for love comes more naturally to the human heart than its opposite." —NELSON MANDELA

Recognize!

In the colloquial language of urban youth, *recognize* is a verb—a command or an expression that means "to understand, to comprehend something that is already known." *Already known*—Black lives have always mattered.

When we were growing up during the 1960s, our parents told us that Black lives mattered. Our lives were important to them, to our extended family, and to our community. No matter what was happening around us, that was a constant truth we were encouraged to embrace. When mean, hurtful words were directed at us, it was true. When our all-Black schools were not supplied with the same resources and materials as schools white children attended, it was true. Even when government agencies and social and cultural institutions declared we were "second-class citizens," it was true. Our Black lives mattered.

Recognize!

Mother Lillian Willis used to say, "Our roots go deep," meaning that there was much about Black life of which to be proud, and a rich legacy from which to draw! She shared stories of family elders and ancestors—how they had overcome, persevered, achieved, and fought for rightful and valued places in the world.

Mother Lurline Hudson would say, "Walk with your head held high." That meant we were SOMEBODY, no matter what others might have said or thought about us. We were special! She sang African American spirituals when she needed reassurance, and she reminded her attentive children that we were made in the image of God. Our lives mattered because God had created us that way. Robbing us of that comforting reality would be difficult.

Recognize!

Our teachers told us that Black lives mattered, too. In their own ways, no matter how facts were distorted or how our history was excluded from textbooks, Black lives mattered. They lifted role models to show us and culled stories and tidbits from Black history to counteract what the books sought to prove: that we did not matter. Because our lives mattered, our teachers said, we had the right to dream, too. Because our lives mattered, we could and would push forward to forge a better future despite seemingly insurmountable hardships.

Unfortunately, the idea of Black lives *not* mattering has been woven into the fabric of our general society. It is a *product* of systemic racism. We encounter it in many places, and we know it when we are confronted by it. We know it by the way some whites respond to Black folks with contempt even though they do not know us personally. They view us through suspicious eyes and with assumptions melded with stereotypes and caricatures. To them, our skin color speaks for us, ahead of us. We know it when we see people who look like us cast aside, pushed down, profiled, held back, jailed or beaten, and, too often, killed. Like George Floyd. Like Breonna Taylor. Like Ahmaud Arbery.

Recognize!

But in Black families, in Black homes, children rise for a new school day and their parents get ready for a workday. Some gather in houses of worship on weekends and play in neighborhood parks on late afternoons. On holidays, Black people gather to celebrate and engage in family love. Achievements and rites of passage are recognized and celebrated with joy at reunions. Black folks go about their daily lives with hope and the expectations for aspirations for successful lives, as do others. That Black lives matter is obvious.

In this anthology, that fact is illuminated by thirty-one award-winning authors and artists of books for young readers. *Recognize!* clearly documents a narrative that Black people have always affirmed and declared: Black lives matter.

The poetry, essays, short stories, and letters cover a broad spectrum of the Black experience—an experience infused with determination, endurance, creativity, pride, and joy as well as struggle. Among them are the brilliant homage to Black storytelling traditions in "The Devil in the Flowers," the affirming words of gender and identity in "Self-Reflection," honoring ancestors in "Claiming My Space," self-affirmation through musical expression in "Drumbeat, Ring Shout, Roll Call, Cypher," a brave teenager's use of a smartphone camera to capture the horrific murder of George Floyd in "Darnella Frazier: Eyewitness," remembering life-altering encounters with police in "The Storms and Sunshine of My Life," the exuberance of Black boy joy in "Joy Lives in You," providing crystal-clear answers to why Black lives matter in "Isn't It Obvious?"

There are excerpts from speeches, poetry, and letters from Black forefathers Frederick Douglass and James Baldwin and Black foremothers Frances Ellen Watkins Harper, Dr. Mary McLeod Bethune, and Daisy Bates, which provide historical context. A thought-provoking essay by activist DeRay Mckesson adds an important perspective from the front lines of the #BlackLivesMatter movement.

Eight outstanding children's book artists have created powerful images that also bear witness to the inherent value of Black life. Rendered in a variety of media from oil painting to collage to digital, the artistic styles provide arresting visual statements that complement the authors' written testimonies.

Recognize! pays homage to Black America's clarion call that all Black lives matter and are precious! It does not matter whether others may think differently. As our mothers and fathers declared, it is so!

Recognize: Black Lives Matter

MIRACLE CHILD

SHARON M. DRAPER

I'm a miracle child
Dressed in brown
I wear cocoa and fudge
And a chocolate gown.

I'm a miracle child
Dressed in tan
I sizzle bronzed steam
In a crunchy baked pan.

I'm a miracle child
Dressed in gold
I'm honey-bright liquid
Sweet in caramel rolled.

I'm a miracle child
Dressed in cream
I'm fluffed and I'm sprinkled
Wrapped in sugar-dipped dream.

I'm a miracle child
Dressed in black
I'm dark sweet licorice—
An ebony-melt snack.

I'm a miracle child
Baked with smiles on my face
I'm grilled to perfection
Dipped in gravy and grace.

I'm a miracle child.

COLORING OUTSIDE THE LINES

Jerdine Nolen

The gift of the children's Bible from a family friend was not new. But it had color pictures to go along with the stories. I could read. I was nine years old. I thumbed through the book. I stared at the pages. There was something about the pictures that didn't seem right—sometimes, I think, it's that way with hand-me-down things.

In our house, Daddy always reads the big family Bible aloud to us. He sits in his big Poppa-sized chair and we sit on the floor at his feet. His booming voice sounds like thunder—a sound just right for reading the Bible. And Daddy loves reading aloud. He is such an actor.

I especially love hearing him read Genesis. He explains what "thou sayeth," "doth," and "beget" this and that means. This book didn't have any of those kinds of words. My three older sisters weren't interested, so the book became mine.

I love *all* kinds of stories. Some I try to memorize, thanks to my fourth-grade teacher, Mrs. Harris, who is also a member of our church. She teaches Sunday School, usually with a map to show where things happened in the world.

We learned about people who lived close to the belt around the earth's waist, the equator. That's where our ancestors came from and the reason for our skin color and our type of hair—the sun is so hot there.

Whenever I get an old/new book, I sleep with it under my pillow. It makes for a bumpy night's sleep, but that way I get to know the book. It's a way to make the old/new book mine.

I always have lots of questions about the things I'm learning. I didn't think my questions were hard, but it seemed most of them were unanswerable. For example, on Sunday in church we talked about Adam and Eve. Mrs. Harris told us *they* were the *first* people. Then in class on Monday Mrs. Harris showed a filmstrip on the cave dwellers that said *they* were the *first* people. I was confused. I raised my hand to ask a question. "If the cave dwellers looked as they did and Adam and Eve looked as they did, *who* came *first*? *Who* were the *first* people?"

My serious question was not meant to cause giggles. Immediately, I got Mrs. Harris's look and pointing index finger. That meant to head for the coatroom in the back of the class. I was glad. It was quiet there. I could think.

I needed answers, even if no one was around to give them to me.

That's when I realized what was wrong with this old/ new book. The people all looked like Dick and Jane, the kids in my reading primer, or people on TV—and they were all white. Even Jesus had white skin and yellow hair. Not one of them fit what Mrs. Harris taught us about what the people living near the equator looked like. They had brown skin and dark hair.

I didn't like the feeling growing inside me. I was feeling like I didn't want the book anymore and I wanted to give it back. Momma and Daddy wouldn't want me to do that. Deep down I really didn't want to. But the pictures were all wrong. I had to do something.

If I was going to read this Bible, I had to make it readable.

Last Saturday, I got a new box of crayons and a new coloring book. I love to color. I always stay in between the lines.

There were only eight colors and the only one that came close enough to the skin color I was looking for was brown—black would hide features, so I used that for the hair.

To keep away from tattle-telling mouths, I worked

on my project in the privacy of my bedroom. But this day, I decided to stretch out on the dining room table just as Daddy was walking by.

"What are you doing to that book?" He picked it up. "This book of *all* books! And it was a gift. . . ."

I had no words. But Daddy had a lot of them. The worst thing about his punishments were the talks.

"We'll talk later."

I prayed to Jesus with the Yellow Hair for almost anything but that. I hoped *he'd* hear me. Daddy's lectures went on forever and sometimes into the next day. The thing was to keep a low profile, stay out of sight. All went well for a while—things quieted down, but not inside of me.

I was already in trouble. I put the book back under my pillow and waited for the house to be quiet.

I grabbed my box of crayons and the Bible and headed for the bathroom. I locked the door behind me. I wouldn't let myself turn back. Sitting on the floor, I opened to the story with Jesus and the little children. I colored them first. Now it was Jesus's turn. After a while, I let out a long yawn and stretched. I packed up all my things. I opened the door and bumped into my father. He was headed for the kitchen for his usual snack. Daddy looked at my hands. I looked at my feet.

What would happen to me now? Had Daddy run out of lectures for me?

"Come near to me," he said. I followed him into the kitchen. "Show me what you were doing with your crayons and that book." I opened my mouth and started to cry. I blurted out everything. "It's not fair. It's not fair! Mrs. Harris says we matter in the world but nobody in this whole book looks like us and the stories take place near the equator where people have darker colored skin like us. See? Everybody in this book looks like the people on TV. Even Jesus has yellow hair."

"What were you doing just now?"

"I couldn't take it, Daddy. I just couldn't take it anymore." I opened the book to Jesus with the No Longer Yellow Hair. "See?"

Daddy looked at the picture for a long time.

"This is what you were doing?"

I nodded. "I wanted this little girl to look like me, and Jesus . . ." I hesitated. ". . . to look like you."

The silence between us was waiting on his answer. Then, Daddy chuckled. "He does kind of favor me."

"And she kind of looks like me, too. Doesn't she?"

Daddy got quiet.

"What are you thinking about?" I asked.

"Hmm . . . thinking about what you did to the book. I see why you did it. I think you had a good reason to do what you did."

"I did."

"Well, I guess nothing left to do than share a slice of Momma's chocolate cake?" Suddenly, we were eating cake, looking at the pages I colored, reading and talking about the stories, and laughing.

Then, Daddy stopped reading.

"Now what?" I asked.

"I'm proud of you." He smiled, hugging me.

"Me too," I answered. "It's just as Mrs. Harris said. Things like this do matter in the world."

WHEN I WAS GROWING UP, I WAS TAUGHT IN AMERICAN HISTORY BOOKS THAT AFRICA HAD NO HISTORY AND NEITHER DID I. THAT I WAS A SAVAGE, ABOUT WHOM THE LESS SAID THE BETTER, WHO HAD BEEN SAVED BY EUROPE AND BROUGHT TO AMERICA. AND, OF COURSE, I BELIEVED IT. I DIDN'T HAVE MUCH CHOICE, THOSE WERE THE ONLY BOOKS THERE WERE.

JAMES BALDWIN'S GREAT DEBATE

WADE HUDSON

James Baldwin looked out at the sea of faces in the auditorium in Cambridge, England. Often in demand to share his views about racial injustice and the treatment of Black people in America, Baldwin was an articulate, moving, and insightful writer and spokesman. That's why he had been invited to speak.

The Cambridge Union Society at Cambridge University had organized a debate on February 18, 1965, with the topic "The American Dream is at the expense of the American Negro." To tackle this challenging subject, they had chosen Baldwin and William F. Buckley.

Buckley was an established magazine editor, political thinker, and founder of the conservative magazine *National Review*. He had made his position about racial equality and justice very clear in a 1957 *National Review* magazine piece entitled "Why the South Must

Prevail." In it he contended that white Southerners were entitled to "take such measures as are necessary to prevail, politically and culturally" over Black Americans.

When the Voting Rights Act of 1965 was passed, which guaranteed Black Americans the right to vote, Buckley said it would result in "chaos" and "mobocratic rule." He also voiced his concerns about other legislation and court rulings that addressed racial segregation in the country.

Baldwin was an acclaimed novelist, essayist, civil rights leader, and political thinker. Born and raised in Harlem, New York, he once recalled, "I knew I was black, of course, but I also knew I was smart. I didn't know how I would use my mind, or even if I could, but that was the only thing I had to use." He began to spend much of his time in libraries, where he found his passion for writing.

Baldwin's first novel, *Go Tell It on the Mountain*, was published in 1953. A semi-autobiography about a fourteen-year-old boy's discovery of his identity during the 1930s, it became a literary classic and established him as an important voice on racial and social issues. He became involved in the civil rights movement in the 1950s and wrote many articles and essays about what was happening in the American South.

Leaders of the Cambridge Union Society felt that

both men were worthy advocates for their positions. A debating and free speech organization, the Society was founded in Cambridge, England, in 1815. It had hosted prominent figures from all areas of public life, including prime ministers and other leaders of state. On this February night in 1965, the auditorium was packed.

James Baldwin spoke first. A short, thin man, he commanded the audience's rapt attention. And as he continued to make his case, members of the audience applauded when points he made resonated with them, which was often.

"When I was growing up, I was taught in American history books that Africa had no history and neither did I," he told them. "That I was a savage, about whom the less said the better, who had been saved by Europe and brought to America. And, of course, I believed it. I didn't have much choice, those were the only books there were."

Baldwin gave vivid examples of how Black Americans had been victimized by racism. He related how Black Americans had helped to build the country and had received little compensation or recognition for their work. When he finished, Baldwin received a prolonged standing ovation. The announcer said he had never seen such a reaction at those events before.

Buckley followed. An accomplished speaker, he

engaged the audience with his intellect and humor. But it was obvious he was on the wrong side of history. Years later, he would change some of his views about civil rights in the United States.

When the debate ended, a vote was taken to determine the winner. Baldwin won, 544 to 164.

The United States of America and countries worldwide are still grappling with race and social justice and the points that Baldwin and Buckley debated in 1965. James Baldwin's books and speeches continue to inspire and inform people today, especially those who are taking steps to do something about those issues.

BLACK LIVES HAVE ALWAYS MATTERED

Wade Hudson

Black lives matter.

Black lives have always mattered.

Our ancestors were kidnapped in Africa, forced to march hundreds of miles, shackled, and bound together.

They were imprisoned in dungeons, forced to wait for the big ships to come—slave ships that would take them on the long, perilous journey across the Atlantic.

Crowded in the hull, they were ill-fed and often beaten. Many died on the way.

Black lives mattered.

Those who survived were paraded to auction blocks in Charleston, Alexandria, and New Orleans and sold o the highest bidder.

the work, the backbreaking labor to bui'

and grow the towns and plantations. They toiled in the fields of cotton and tobacco from sunup to sundown.

Fathers, mothers, and children were sold and separated from their families, never to see each other again.

Their tears of pain and separation were met with the whip and the lash.

Black lives mattered then, too.

That's why so many resisted as best they could.

Harriet Tubman escaped but went back south many times, facing sure death if caught, to bring her people to freedom.

The abolitionists Frederick Douglass and Sojourner Truth dedicated their lives to break the chains of slavery.

Journalist Ida B. Wells-Barnett crusaded against the lynching of Black people in the South.

Educators Booker T. Washington started Tuskegee Institute and Dr. Mary McLeod Bethune established Bethune-Cookman when there were few schools for Black students.

The attorneys Thurgood Marshall and Constance Baker Motley went to the U.S. Supreme Court to change laws that discriminated against their people.

They all knew Black lives mattered.

Everywhere, in the North, in the South, in the East, and in the West, in towns and in cities, decade by decade, centuries long, wherever Black people were . .

Black Lives Mattered.

When fighting in wars to support their country.

When creating the inventions that make life easier and better.

When producing the literature, music, dances, and art of our culture.

When achieving great feats in sports.

Black lives mattered.

Rosa Parks knew this was true when she refused to give up her seat on a segregated bus.

So did the civil rights leaders Fannie Lou Hamer, Martin Luther King, Jr., and Malcolm X.

Black lives mattered in 1955 when Emmett Till was murdered in Mississippi and when four little girls were killed in a Birmingham church in 1963.

Just as it mattered when Eric Garner, Trayvon Martin, Michael Brown, Tamir Rice, Sandra Bland, Breonna Taylor, and George Floyd lost their lives to white brutality and indifference.

Black lives have always mattered to Black people.

We love and hug, sing and dance, laugh and joke, tell tall tales, rap, and play our instruments.

We shout our praises in houses of worship, celebrate our achievements, push each other forward, and desire to live each day to the fullest measure!

The image of the horrible murder of George Floyd was too much for others.

Viewing callous shootings opened their eyes.
See the protest signs?
Hear the marching feet?
Listen to the chants!
Black lives matter!
Black lives matter!
Black lives matter!
Black lives will always matter!

FAMOUS BLERDS IN HISTORY

KEITH KNIGHT

MAE JEMISON was the first Black woman to travel into space, serving on the Space Shuttle Endeavour!!
Far out!!
ROBERT SMALLS cosplayed as a Confederate sea captain, stole a Confederate gunboat & sailed his family to freedom!!
Smalls was HUGE!!
LONNIE JOHNSON was an engineer for NASA who invented the Super Soaker water gun in 1990!
Made quite a splash!!
So...what do you wanna do now?
Change the world!!
But first, we soak Mom & Dad!!
SUPAH SOAKA

WHEN JACKIE ROBINSON LOOSENED HIS FIST AND TURNED THE OTHER CHEEK, HE WAS TAKING THE BLOWS FOR THE LOVE AND FUTURE OF HIS PEOPLE.

HANK AARON PASSES ON THE LEGACY

WADE HUDSON

On April 8, 1974, a sellout crowd of 53,775 packed Atlanta Fulton County Stadium hoping to witness history. Three days earlier, Henry Aaron had hit a home run to tie Babe Ruth's historic Major League Baseball record of 714 career home runs. Most baseball fans thought the record that had stood for thirty-seven years would never be broken. Now, with one swing of the bat, a Black player could surpass the total amassed by the man many considered the greatest to ever play the game. Babe Ruth was an icon, a national hero of America's favorite pastime, baseball.

In the fourth inning, a determined and focused Aaron took the first pitch for a ball. On the second offering, he sent the ball soaring over the left field wall more than 330 feet away. Fans who were at the game and millions who were following on television and radio had gotten their wish.

When the new home run king reached home plate after circling the bases, he was mobbed by his teammates. Fireworks were set off, and an eleven-minute celebration ensued. Georgia governor Jimmy Carter, soon-to-be president, hurried to the field to congratulate him.

But there were those who didn't want a Black man to break Major League Baseball's career home run record. Aaron had faced racism all his life, but nothing compared to the continuous taunts and thousands of hate letters he received as he pursued Babe Ruth's record. Threats against Aaron's life were constant. A bodyguard had to be assigned to accompany him wherever he went.

Henry Louis Aaron was more than a baseball player. He was a civil rights leader who spoke out against inequality and discrimination, donated to civil rights causes, and established foundations to assist needy kids. He was determined to follow the example set by a man he admired, Jackie Robinson, who in 1947 became the first Black man to play Major League Baseball in the modern era.

In an op-ed published in the *New York Times* in 1997, Aaron shared his concerns about baseball's failure to honor Robinson's 1947 heroic feat. He also admonished Black athletes during that time for not following Robinson's example of fighting for social justice.

"We were on a mission," he wrote. "And, although Willie Mays, Ernie Banks, Frank Robinson, Willie Stargell, Lou Brock, Bob Gibson and I were trying to make our marks individually, we understood that we were on a collective mission. Jackie Robinson demonstrated to us that, for a black player in our day and age, true success could not be an individual thing."

In 2004, because of continuous pressure from Henry Aaron, Jackie Robinson's family, and others, Major League Baseball finally recognized Robinson by formally instituting Jackie Robinson Day each April 15, the day Jackie broke the color line.

Today, many Black athletes follow Robinson's and Aaron's examples by lending their voice and support to the movement for social justice, including Colin Kaepernick, LeBron James, Maya Moore, Carmelo Anthony, Renee Montgomery, Chris Paul, and members of the Women's National Basketball Association.

Henry Aaron passed away at age eighty-six on January 21, 2021. In a Twitter post, Kaepernick, a former National Football League quarterback who had taken a knee several years earlier to protest social injustice, wrote, "Hank Aaron has always been a giant—a living legend—whose courage, resilience, & honor inspired millions. He fought for us with every swing of his bat & paved the way for us to walk in. I was fortunate enough to be able to tell him 'thank you' in person. Rest in Power Hammerin' Hank."

THE STORMS AND SUNSHINE OF MY LIFE

Lamar Giles

I once saw several police officers in full riot gear come to the rescue of a white teenaged lifeguard. They were "saving" the *lifeguard* from an eleven-year-old Black boy who had *yelled* at him.

I'm serious.

I was nineteen years old, working as a gym attendant at my local community center—the same community center I'd frequented my entire life. It was the first place I remembered swimming. The first place I'd lobbed a basketball at a rim I couldn't quite hit. There I was, watching someone so like me at age eleven facing off with grown, armed men. How things escalated to that point is both a longer story and somewhat irrelevant. You've heard the summary before: a Black person talked back to a white person.

The Black boy never touched the lifeguard—I know because I got between them when voices got loud. The Black boy was never a credible threat to the lifeguard. He was roughly six years younger, six inches shorter, and sixty pounds lighter. Yet, fear of Black skin and a sense of being disrespected triggered a 911 call and the arrival of a bunch of RoboCop-looking officers with hands on holsters. That Black boy, along with several of his buddies, got kicked out of the community center during a classic Virginia summer storm with no way home.

That same evening, I quit my job (not before throwing my gym keys at the feet of the lifeguard and our boss—who'd been celebrating the expulsion of those kids like they'd just scored a touchdown—and calling them both some colorful names on my way out). Then I crammed those kids, maybe five of them, into my tiny car and drove them home in the rain. That they all fit just shows how small they were. So small and already part of a terrible club that I also belonged to.

My experience with police officers is a mixed bag—the mix being "bad" and "worse." I was eleven when a cop rung our doorbell in the middle of the night looking for a young car thief and coerced my stepdad into (a) proving I wasn't the thief and (b) allowing a search (without a warrant) of my bedroom to ensure I wasn't hiding the thief because the officer figured we might be friends. (We weren't.) I was in Ninja Turtle pajamas while he shined a flashlight under my bed. I remember *that* clearly, though I'm a little fuzzy on the first time a police officer drew his gun on me and my friends.

I mean, I remember *every* time it happened, but it happened so often that I now get the instances confused. Was the first time when we'd gone to a basketball tournament in Fort Lee and MPs wielding the big *Call of Duty* guns pulled us over to make sure we weren't "getting into trouble"? Was it the time a white lady told the cops a group of scary Black guys were following her, so they pulled me and my friends over, daring us to make a move so they could beat us down (or worse)? Was it the time we were at a party and a cop rolled up, gun already drawn, because of a noise complaint? Or was it—

You get the idea.

In my town it occurred enough that I don't recall being frightened by the prospect of something tragic happening. It was more like, "Here we go again." Because some of the people with badges were also bullies who liked reminding us what they could do and get away with. For them, harassing and threatening us was fun. For us, it was as inevitable as those loud and frequent summer storms we knew to expect.

What follows storms, though? Sunshine. Eventually. I can remember every time I stared down the barrel of some cop's gun. But those horrible moments are not what I remember most. About my youth, or my friends.

What I remember most is winning a writing contest in fourth grade and sensing it was maybe the first step toward something important and great. I recall with great clarity being the good kind of scared that came from watching horror movies I was too young to see with my big cousins who didn't care that I was a fifth grader. In seventh grade I began my first lessons in finance by only spending half my lunch money in the cafeteria and using the other half to buy new comic books on Wednesdays. I remember eleventh grade when my school's basketball team almost won States and how my friends on that team were determined to take another crack at excellence the following year. I remember our senior trip, riding a bus across five states to visit Disney World, where the late, great Aaliyah put on a concert. She told us from the stage, "I'm one of you. I'm class of '97, too!" I'm certain half of Florida heard our cheers.

I remember those things the most because I didn't let being terrorized by a bully with a badge define me. Yet, I know I'm lucky because not all of us get to go on, unscathed, to life's joys. Not Tamir. Not Philando. Not Breonna.

Black. Lives. Matter. So do Black Voices. And

Black Joy. Speak out against those who terrorize our community, like Patrisse Cullors, Alicia Garza, and Opal Tometi did when they founded BLM. Take the opportunities your talent affords you to bring awareness to those who cause pain in our community, like Colin Kaepernick did when he took a knee. But also hug your family and laugh with your friends, and learn that new dance (even if you're a bad dancer like me) the way only you can.

Because if/when you need to offer a hand to new members of this club of ours, you can assure them, from experiences both great and terrible, that those inevitable storms don't last.

AT OUR KITCHEN TABLE

LESA CLINE-RANSOME

At our kitchen table
we bow our heads
in blessing
of an abundance
of family
food
and conversation
rising as fiercely
as the storms of
sickness and unrest
gather
outside our door

At our kitchen table
over braised short ribs
roasted potatoes and sautéed spinach

we scoop seconds
and wonder
how bird-watching
and dog walking
become
sporting season
on Black men
in Central Park

At our kitchen table
we scrape our plates clean
of white beans and smoked turkey
and marvel at friends and allies who
step up
step out
speak up
call out
the
All Lives-ing
Blue Lives-ing
Whatabout-ing
Both sides-ing
folks who see
red, white, and blue
but are blind to
the lives of
Black and brown

At our kitchen table
we swallow
lemon shrimp
and pasta
tossed with parsley
and force down the
bitter taste of
name after name
night after night
flashed across the screen
Ahmaud
Breonna
George
Jacob
as we sit swallowing
heaping helpings of
hurt
pain
rage
onto our plates

At our kitchen table
we wipe our chins
of warm triple-berry cobbler
and vanilla ice cream
and savor the sweetness
of legend

John Lewis
living a life of good trouble
in Atlanta
in Selma
in Washington, DC,
across the Edmund Pettus Bridge
gone now
his spirit
still marching us
forward

At our kitchen table
we gather to
shed tears
offer prayers
send money
write letters
draw posters
make plans
until we too
rise up
as a family and
step out
to walk
to shout
in protest

Do
You
See
Us
Now

After
Days
Weeks
Months
of the world
tearing us to pieces
it is our talk
of hurt and history
rage and resistance
at our kitchen table
that makes us all
whole again

ISN'T IT OBVIOUS?

Nic Stone

The first time I heard the phrase "Black Lives Matter," I wasn't sure what to really *think*. It was mid-2013, and initially, the words felt funny on my tongue. Tasted weird. Had a bizarre texture. Not because I disagreed with them. But because, strung together, they seemed like something that would make a person say: *Thank you, Captain Obvious.*

Of course Black lives mattered. Every life matters.

But the more I heard and saw it, the more I started to wonder: *What is making people feel the need to say that?*

In truth, back then, I wasn't much of a news watcher. I had just moved back to the United States from Israel, and it seemed like American news stations focused solely on gloom-and-doom stories. After living for three years in a country where people were consistently worried about the potential for a sudden outbreak of war, the last thing I needed while trying to settle back into my own home country was more news-related stress.

While I was still in Israel, I'd heard about two different boys—both African American—who'd been killed by adults with guns in the United States. Trayvon Martin was shot by a man who assumed Trayvon was up to no good in a neighborhood where Trayvon had every right to be. And Jordan Davis was shot over loud music in a convenience store parking lot by a man in the next car.

Both boys were unarmed, and both men who pulled the triggers appeared to be white. I was deeply unsettled by the idea of grown men killing teenaged boys because the men assumed the boys were dangerous.

I remember asking myself: *Who decided that a kid in a hoodie or one listening to loud music is automatically* dangerous? *What would give these men the impression that these* children *were any sort of threat?*

So I thought about it, but I didn't think *too* much about it. It was honestly too tough a pill to swallow: Black teenage boys being deemed threatening just because they were teenagers who happened to be Black . . . I didn't want to accept that as a possibility.

Especially since between the deaths of Trayvon Martin and Jordan Davis, I gave birth to a Black boy of my own.

But that phrase kept popping up. *Black Lives Matter.* Usually without spaces between the words and with what we oldies used to call a "pound sign" attached at the front: *#BlackLivesMatter.* There was something going on. And I needed to get to the bottom of it.

I learned that the hashtag was created by three Black women—Alicia Garza, Opal Tometi, and Patrisse Cullors—who were outraged that the man who killed Trayvon Martin was declared not guilty in court.

I was also outraged.

The phrase began to make more sense.

Seven months later, almost to the day, a mistrial was declared on the murder charge in the case against the man who'd killed Jordan Davis.

I was outraged again. And Black Lives Matter echoed in my mind.

Six months after *that*, an eighteen-year-old unarmed Black boy was shot and killed in Missouri by a police officer.

It became crystal clear that there was a genuine *problem*, and Black Lives Matter went from a slogan posted on social media to a bold declaration printed on T-shirts and to a plea printed on signs as people took to the streets in protest.

"People" including me.

Three months after *that*, a twelve-year-old playing with a pellet gun was killed—also by a police officer.

None of the police officers involved were charged with a crime.

I got louder with *my* use of the rallying cry then: started wearing my T-shirts to the grocery store and put a decal on my car. Because I knew then what I know now: it *isn't* obvious that Black lives matter. That Black people—especially Black children—are immeasurably valuable members of American society.

As of my writing this, it's been nine and a half years since the death of Trayvon Martin, and just over eight since the birth of *#BlackLivesMatter.*

And we're still saying it.

Because stuff still happening—an unarmed Black man murdered while out for a run, another unarmed Black man pinned to the ground by a police officer's knee until he died, a Black woman shot to death while *sleeping* when police stormed her apartment and opened fire . . . (and those officers weren't charged for harming her)—

So we have to *keep* saying it. Keep reminding people.

And keep reminding ourselves.

Because even if it seems like society still hasn't gotten it, it's true: Black people have infinite power and magic and light and love to offer the world.

Black.

Lives.

Matter.

HE IS NOT HERS, ALTHOUGH SHE BORE

FOR HIM A MOTHER'S PAINS;

HE IS NOT HERS, ALTHOUGH HER BLOOD

IS COURSING THROUGH HIS VEINS!

••••••

"The Slave Mother" first appeared in Frances Ellen Watkins Harper's second poetry collection entitled *Poems on Miscellaneous Subjects*, published in 1854. Her first collection was published in 1845 when she was just twenty years old. Harper continued to write poetry, essays, short stories, and novels throughout her life. "The Slave Mother" illustrates one of the cruelest aspects of slavery, the separation of children from their parents and being sold to different masters.

THE SLAVE MOTHER

FRANCES ELLEN WATKINS HARPER

Heard you that shriek? It rose
　　So wildly on the air,
It seemed as if a burden'd heart
　　Was breaking in despair.

Saw you those hands so sadly
　　clasped—
　　The bowed and feeble head—
The shuddering of that fragile form—
　　That look of grief and dread?

Saw you the sad, imploring eye?
　　Its every glance was pain,
As if a storm of agony
　　Were sweeping through the brain.

She is a mother pale with fear,
    Her boy clings to her side,
And in her kirtle vainly tries
    His trembling form to hide.

He is not hers, although she bore
    For him a mother's pains;
He is not hers, although her blood
    Is coursing through his veins!

He is not hers, for cruel hands
    May rudely tear apart
The only wreath of household love
    That binds her breaking heart.

His love has been a joyous light
    That o'er her pathway smiled,
A fountain gushing ever new,
    Amid life's desert wild.

His lightest word has been a tone
    Of music round her heart,
Their lives a streamlet blent in one—
    Oh, Father! must they part?

They tear him from her circling arms,
    Her last and fond embrace.

Oh! never more may her sad eyes
  Gaze on his mournful face.

No marvel, then, these bitter shrieks
  Disturb the listening air:
She is a mother, and her heart
  Is breaking in despair.

JOY LIVES IN YOU

KELLY STARLING LYONS

Dear Josh,

Do you remember how excited you were about going to your friend's fifth-grade graduation party at the park? You couldn't wait for an epic water battle with your boys. This was going to be your first socially distanced hangout after months of being cooped up.

The week before the gathering, we looked online for a water squirter that would be cool but not too realistic. You know toy guns are off-limits in our family. We talk about news stories that show Black boys being seen as threats instead of treasures.

"How does that make you feel?" I ask.

"It's not fair," you reply with hurt clouding your eyes.

Fair. Each time you say that word, it hits me in the heart. You're right. It's not fair. It's shameful and heartbreaking, devastating and wrong. Racism is a weight you shouldn't have to bear.

Yet I know you'll face bigotry countless times throughout your life. There are people who will make snap judgments about you based on hate and stereotypes. They won't see the trash-talking gamer who loves to ride his bike, write Star Wars fan fiction, and shoot hoops. They won't see your sweetness and sense of wonder, just their own twisted fears.

Injustice will creep out when you least expect it. Like the time your question was snubbed on a field trip, but the ones from your white friends were answered. Like the time you and your sibling were in a gift shop checking out the toys and a saleswoman kept hovering nearby. Like the time some boys you thought were friends called you the N-word.

In those moments, you must embrace who you are harder than ever before. In those moments, you must look inside and know you are a blessing. Beauty shines in you, in your family and friends, in the ancestors who paved the way and light your path. When someone tries to shrink your spirit, stand tall and soar. Speak your truth. Bring it with your brilliance. Fight back with your fierce commitment to justice.

It won't always be easy. There will be days that make you want to moan and days that fill your soul with song. You come from a long line of warriors, dreamers, writers and artists, innovators, scientists, and change makers. That's an army inside of you. When you're feeling low, rally the troops and lift your voice. Love and hope beat hate every time.

Call on your other superpower, too. Joy heals and strengthens, like a hug after a want-to-curl-up-and-pull-the-covers-over-my-head kind of day. It lives in you and swirls all around.

I see it when you're playing chess with your granddad, pumping your fist when you win and taking mental notes when you don't. I see it when you ride your bike with your dad, pedaling into the whispering wind, confident and proud. I see it when your grandmothers or sibling say something funny and your eyes crinkle and your laughter floats like a bunch of balloons sailing to the sky.

That day in the park, masks couldn't dim the bliss of you and your friends. It gleamed in your sparkling eyes. To people passing by, it may have just looked like you were having a bit of afternoon fun. But for me, listening to your glee-filled shouts and seeing your brown legs dipping and darting from the aim of icy water, it was something else—asserting your right to be happy and carefree.

Each day, you make this world better with your genius, kindness, and determination. If joy had a face, it would be a mirror showing your smile. Remember who you are when times get hard:

Black.
Beautiful.
Loved.

Always,
Mommy

WITNESS

Nikki Grimes

From the world wide window
of my computer screen,
I witness peaceful protest
momentarily overshadowed
by itchy fingered vandals
damaging storefronts
then hiding among the crowd.
An ebony warrior woman
storms the street,
chastising lazy looters.
A microphone rudely shoved
in her face,
she carefully loads her words
like bullets
shoots straight

at the screen
to tell the white world
through clenched teeth
that, fortunately, we are
hungrier for equality
than revenge.
Beyond exhaustion
she nevertheless
lines up her dreams
like soldiers
ready to march another day
for victory.
Mother, your children see
    you
and are grateful
for your fierceness.
Keep fueling their
    tomorrows.
Full freedom
is just up ahead.

YOU ARE . . .

DENENE MILLNER

They say little girls are made of sugar and spice
and everything nice
and that is sweet and all

But Black girls—oh, Black girls,
you are so much more . . .

More like diamonds, I say.

That good Black?
That brown sugar sweet, sweet?
It is precious—
created under extreme pressure and high
*   temperature,*
deep down in the way down, you see.

It is . . .

hunching between your mama's knees while she
twists your hair into a glorious crown . . .

and marching down the aisle early Sunday
morning, singing, Hosannah! *while the*
deaconesses deal with the tambourines on the
twos and the fours.

It is . . .

weaving like lightning between the double-Dutch
ropes
Bluebells/cockleshells/easy, ivy over . . .

and getting the first taste of Auntie's sweet potato
pie, made from scratch, from memory, just like
her mama's and her mama's before that—just
like yours will be.

It is . . .

being loud or quiet and regular or bold and
colorful or understated, or all of them at
once or none of them at all or whatever you
choose . . .

*and knowing, too, that a bunch of stamps cannot
and will not ever be big enough to cover over
your intelligence, ability, intentions, mettle,
light, or heart.*

It is . . .

*knowing the genius of Beyoncé and Rihanna and
Mary and Nina and Billie and Zora and Ida
and Nikki and Audre and Assata and Alice
and Toni, understanding that each of them
speak to you, through you, for you, because they
love you . . .*

*and learning to love that brown skin and every last
one of those curves and all the bends in that
kinky hair and all that rah-rah with all your
might because that is what it will take to know
that you are good enough, pretty enough, smart
enough, big enough, tough enough, right enough,
fierce enough . . .*

Enough.

*Brilliantly so . . . full stop.
No exceptions.
No takebacks.*

No matter what anybody has to say about it.
No matter what anybody has to say.

You simply . . . are.

Uniquely, beautifully, perfectly, divinely so.

IS IT NOT ASTONISHING THAT, WHILE WE ARE
PLOWING, PLANTING, AND REAPING, USING ALL
KINDS OF MECHANICAL TOOLS, ERECTING HOUSES,
CONSTRUCTING BRIDGES, BUILDING SHIPS . . . WHILE
WE ARE READING, WRITING, AND CIPHERING, ACTING
AS CLERKS, MERCHANTS, AND SECRETARIES, HAVING
AMONG US LAWYERS, DOCTORS, MINISTERS, POETS,
AUTHORS, EDITORS, ORATORS, AND TEACHERS;
THAT WE ARE ENGAGED IN ALL THE ENTERPRISES
COMMON TO OTHER MEN . . . LIVING, MOVING,
ACTING, THINKING, PLANNING, LIVING IN FAMILIES AS
HUSBANDS, WIVES, AND CHILDREN, AND, ABOVE ALL,
CONFESSING AND WORSHIPPING THE CHRISTIAN'S GOD,
AND LOOKING HOPEFULLY FOR LIFE AND IMMORTALITY
BEYOND THE GRAVE—WE ARE CALLED UPON TO PROVE
THAT WE ARE MEN?

Frederick Douglass delivered this speech in 1852 before a crowd of nearly six hundred men and women at the newly constructed Corinthian Hall in Rochester, New York. The Rochester Ladies' Anti-Slavery Society had invited Douglass to speak on the anniversary of the signing of the Declaration of Independence (July 4, 1776); Douglass chose instead to speak on July 5. He was aware that on the same date twenty-five years earlier, thousands of African Americans had paraded down Broadway in New York City in celebration of the official end of slavery in New York State.

When Douglass gave his speech, the United States was engaged in a fierce struggle over the institution of slavery.

At that time, more than 3 million African Americans were held in bondage. Just two years before, the U.S. Congress had enacted the Fugitive Slave Law of 1850, which required that all escaped slaves, upon capture, be returned to their masters. Officials and citizens of free states were required to cooperate. All of these issues were apparently on Douglass's mind when he approached the podium on July 5, 1852, at Corinthian Hall.

WHAT TO THE SLAVE IS THE FOURTH OF JULY?

ROCHESTER, NEW YORK, 1852

FREDERICK DOUGLASS

Fellow-citizens, above your national, tumultuous joy, I hear the mournful wail of millions, whose chains, heavy and grievous yesterday, are, today, rendered more intolerable by the jubilant shouts that reach them. If I do forget, if I do not faithfully remember those bleeding children of sorrow this day, "may my right hand forget her cunning, and may my tongue cleave to the roof of my mouth!"

To forget them, to pass lightly over their wrongs, and to chime in with the popular theme, would be treason most scandalous and shocking, and would make me a reproach before God and the world.

My subject, then, fellow-citizens, is "American Slavery." I shall see this day and its popular characteristics from the slave's point of view. Standing here, identified with the American bondman, making his wrongs mine, I do not hesitate to declare, with all my soul, that the character and conduct of this nation never looked blacker to me than on this Fourth of July!

Whether we turn to the declarations of the past, or to the professions of the present, the conduct of the nation seems equally hideous and revolting. America is false to the past, false to the present, and solemnly binds herself to be false to the future. Standing with God and the crushed and bleeding slave on this occasion, I will, in the name of humanity which is outraged, in the name of liberty which is fettered, in the name of the Constitution and the Bible, which are disregarded and trampled upon, dare to call in question and to denounce, with all the emphasis I can command, everything that serves to perpetuate slavery—the great sin and shame of America! "I will not equivocate—I will not excuse." I will use the severest language I can command, and yet not one word shall escape me that any man, whose judgment is not blinded by prejudice, or who is not at heart a slave-holder, shall not confess to be right and just.

But I fancy I hear some of my audience say it is just in this circumstance that you and your brother Abolitionists fail to make a favorable impression on the public mind. Would you argue more, and denounce less, would you persuade more and rebuke less, your cause would be much more likely to succeed. But, I submit, where all is plain there is nothing to be argued. What point in the anti-slavery creed would you have me argue? On what branch of the subject do the people of this country need light? Must I undertake to prove that the slave is a man? That point is conceded already. Nobody doubts it. The slave-holders themselves acknowledge it in the enactment of laws for their government. They acknowledge it when they punish disobedience on the part of the slave. There are seventy-two crimes in the State of Virginia, which, if committed by a black man (no matter how ignorant he be), subject him to the punishment of death; while only two of these same crimes will subject a white man to the like punishment.

What is this but the acknowledgment that the slave is a moral, intellectual, and responsible being? The manhood of the slave is conceded. It is admitted in the fact that Southern statute books are covered with enactments forbidding, under severe fines and penalties, the teaching of the slave to read and write. When you can point to any such laws, in reference to the beasts of the field, then I may consent to argue the manhood of the slave. When the dogs in your streets, when the fowls of the air, when the cattle on your hills, when the fish of the sea, and the reptiles that crawl, shall be unable to distinguish the slave from a brute, *then* will I argue with you that the slave is a man!

For the present, it is enough to affirm the equal manhood of the Negro race. Is it not astonishing that, while we are plowing, planting, and reaping, using all kinds of mechanical tools, erecting houses, constructing bridges, building ships, working in metals of brass, iron, copper, silver and gold; that, while we are reading, writing, and ciphering, acting as clerks, merchants, and secretaries, having among us lawyers, doctors, ministers, poets, authors, editors, orators, and teachers; that we are engaged in all the enterprises common to other men—digging gold in California, capturing the whale in the Pacific, feeding sheep and cattle on the hillside, living, moving, acting, thinking, planning, living in families as husbands, wives, and children, and, above all, confessing and worshipping the Christian's God, and looking hopefully for life and immortality beyond the grave—we are called upon to prove that we are men?

BLACK BOY READING

Ronald L. Smith

When I was a kid—maybe your age—my dad was in the Air Force, which meant we moved around a lot.

I was born in Maine, which is in New England. New England is a group of states made up of Maine, Vermont, New Hampshire, Connecticut, Rhode Island, and Massachusetts.

I remember being depressed and sad every time we moved to a new Air Force base. *I just made friends*, I would tell my mom and dad as the car backed out of our driveway, *and now I have to leave them behind.*

Believe me, moving to a new school every two years wasn't fun.

But now when I look back on it, I'm glad of the experience. I got to see a lot of the world as a kid. We lived in Japan, Michigan, South Carolina, Illinois,

Alabama, Delaware, and Washington, DC, to name a few places.

We didn't have the internet back then. No Instagram. No TikTok. No Snapchat. Can you imagine that? We had to find other ways to entertain ourselves. And that's exactly what we did.

My brothers and I climbed pecan trees in Alabama and scrambled down with hands full of nuts, the twisted, rough branches scratching our knees and elbows. We jumped from the roof of our house in Michigan to land in giant snowdrifts. And, of course, being kids, we thought we were invincible, so we raced our bikes down Dead Man's Hill in South Carolina. Fortunately, none of us ever got seriously hurt.

One thing I remember about living on Air Force bases is the ear-piercing wail of sirens that would go off unexpectedly day and night. They were emergency preparedness tests, just in case there was ever a national disaster. A loud and cold mechanical voice would come on after, giving us the all-clear. When it was over, we used to run outside and stare up at the sky, expecting to see a UFO or a giant plane with blinking lights coming in for a landing.

Even though moving was tough, there was one thing that always helped: exploring the library at a new school. There, I didn't have to worry about leaving my friends. I could find new friends in books.

Books like *The Hobbit*, The Chronicles of Narnia, and *The Wonderful Flight to the Mushroom Planet*. I read *R Is for Rocket* and *S Is for Space* by the science fiction writer Ray Bradbury. I loved these books and many more. They allowed me to explore new worlds, people, places, and things.

My brother and I loved fantasy stories so much, we used to draw maps of imaginary worlds, inspired by the ones we found in our favorite books. We wanted them to look real, with torn edges and scorch marks, like some explorer had just discovered them on a deserted island. So, you know what we did? We put them in the oven. That's right.

In the oven.

Paper.

On a cookie sheet.

It's a good thing we never burned the house down.

I remember long ago—I think it was in Maine—a poet came to our school. His name was Philip Booth, and he had written a rhyming picture book called *Crossing*, which was all about trains traveling through small towns. Something about the poem ignited a passion in me for the way words *worked*. The rhythm and sound of the words filled my head with pictures and questions. Years later, I found out that the book used something called onomatopoeia. Yikes. Big word. *Onomatopoeia* is using words that actually imitate the sound that a thing makes. Have you ever heard of Rice Krispies cereal? There was a TV commercial that used the words *snap, crackle,* and *pop.* Those words are the sounds you hear when you pour the milk over the cereal. Think about the sounds an animal makes: *moo, howl, meow, hiss.* What about water? *Splash, drip, plop.* These are all words that use onomatopoeia.

I loved that book called *Crossing* so much that I memorized it. I also memorized poems from *The Lord of the Rings.* But there was something missing in those stories. I didn't realize it as a kid. It came to me much later. You see, those books didn't have any characters in them who looked like me. When I wrote my first novel, *Hoodoo,* I wanted a little Black boy to be the main character, so that's what I did.

Every kid deserves to see themselves in a story. No matter who they are. Maybe there's another Air Force kid who, right now, is moving from state to state, losing friends and making new ones. If that's you, I hope you find stories that will stay with you forever, too, like they have for me.

<hr />

One final note. Don't do any of the crazy stuff I did when I was a kid, like riding your bike down hills, jumping off the roof, or putting paper in an oven. I got very lucky that I was never hurt!

SELF-REFLECTION

KWAME MBALIA

I'm a student sitting in the back of the class. You probably know someone like me. In Washington, DC, I'm a girl. In Memphis, a boy. In North Carolina, I'm wrestling with the idea of gender. Everywhere, across the nation, there's a student like me. We're Black and we've been paying attention to the news, and the internet, and the whispered conversations our parents have when they think we're asleep, or that teachers have in hallways between classes. I've been listening. I know more than you think I do. I've been quiet so far.

But not for long.

My school could be in Los Angeles, or Portland, or Raleigh, or just outside of Chicago. It's in an old building with trailers to accommodate all the new students, or maybe it's a new magnet school built in the last few years. I love my teachers. They push me, encourage me, stick up for me. They take the realities of the day and turn them into something called a teachable moment. They've thrown out funky old reading lists and replaced them with books like *Long Way Down* and *Brown Girl Dreaming* and *New Kid* and *Ways to Make Sunshine*. This is a new year.

"Okay, everyone," my teacher calls out from the front of the room. "Your first assignment, Self-Reflection, is due. Come place them on my desk and then take out your chosen reading text. We'll start English and Language Arts in a few minutes."

Book bags unzip, papers rustle, and the quiet hum of activity fills the room. Friends swap jokes, handshakes, and snacks. Students file past the assignment bin and deposit projects ranging from essays to poems to sketches. They're all so good. We were supposed to capture what we're feeling. That thing inside. What our emotions would look like if someone peeked inside us. I see some projects that look like a goal, something far-off like a career, while in others, family legacy shines through.

I'm the last in line to hand in my work. I can't help but feel scared. Shy. I'm not sure if what I did will make sense. If the teacher will get it. My chest feels tight. Everything screams for me to give an excuse, to ask for more time, to try to do something else. Then the teacher meets my eye and the line is moving forward. I'm five students away from the front.

One student hands in an essay on climate change trapped in their lungs. Someone else has drawn a picture of their block, with graves beneath luxury apartment buildings. Two students, siblings, collaborated on a mural and brought in high-resolution photos of their assignment. It shows a giant tree stretching from cracked concrete. It bears fruit with brown children inside. Beneath the tree's limbs, a crowd of their great-uncles and aunts and grandparents water massive roots from a watering can labeled *History*.

Now I'm two students away.

One student seems to be empty-handed, until he takes off his large bulky sweater to reveal a T-shirt he airbrushed. On the front, a group of Black children run away, their mouths wide-open in laughter as tears of joy stream down their faces. They're playing a game, tag maybe, or hide-and-seek. But on the back of the shirt, that same group of children run, their mouths open in a scream, crying, fear written in their expressions. Neither side reveals who is chasing them.

Now I'm in front of the teacher, unsure and hesitant.

"Yes?" the teacher says, smiling. "Do you have your assignment?"

I nod.

"Excellent! Put it here and then go grab your book."

I take a deep breath. Softly, I drop a single white piece of paper, slightly wrinkled from how tight my hands gripped it, into the bin facedown. I exhale, as if a weight has been removed from my shoulders, as if my fate is out of my hands now, but I don't move. I can't. I need to make sure the teacher sees it. Sees me. I don't know why, but it's the most important thing in the world right now.

The teacher flips over the paper, pauses. Stares.

It's a picture of me. My mouth is stretched open in a frozen shout of anger, frustration, and rage. But this isn't a pencil sketch, a watercolor, or even a charcoal rendition.

No.

Names outline my face. Chants and hashtags define my expression. Breonna Taylor's name forms my ear, George Floyd the chin. Trayvon and Tamir frame my eyes. #SayHerName, #ICan'tBreathe, #StopKillingUs—words repeated over and over, fruitlessly so far, color in my eyebrows. And in the mouth, defining the tip of the tongue, I wrote my own name.

This is what I see every morning when I wake up. When I pass the mirror and look at my reflection.

72

Faces, like my own, in the newspaper. On the television. Online, at school assemblies, in magazines. Faces that could be me.

Slowly, carefully, the teacher meets my eyes and says . . .

BLACK BUTTERFLY

PAULA CHASE

Most people know the story of Sleeping Beauty and how a bitter fairy, mad because she was overlooked, cursed Princess Aurora, so that when the princess turned sixteen, she'd prick her finger and die. Until the Lilac Fairy softened the curse by making Aurora go into a deep sleep instead.

I am Aurora, pricked not by an old-timey spindle but by a screenshot.

And just like the Lilac Fairy, my mother's words wrapped around me, trying to protect. "Look, Lila, don't hate, motivate. Because the energy you use to hate will drag you down."

I nodded, lips pressed tight to fight the tears that were swelling my throat and scratching at the back of my eyes. I wanted to put my face in her lap and cry until the hurt washed away. Instead, I obeyed like I was supposed to. Ballerinas are good at doing what is asked of us. Even when it's hard.

Like standing tall until our spines are clicked into place as if someone put it together with building blocks. Like leaping and turning on command. Like ignoring a screenshot of a private chat that punches a hole in your heart so deep, you can hardly breathe.

DruBoo: She's a good dancer

JayceInURFace: IDC she's only been here 2 years 🙄 One of us should have got the lead and you know it, Dru. #10YearClub

Rip-Ah-DaStar: Guise chill. She's a diversity pick.

DruBoo: Good is good, Jayce.

JayceInURFace: diversity pick? 🤮

DruBoo: 😒

Rip-Ah-DaStar: They probably HAD to pick a black dancer

JayceInURFace: Had to?

Rip-Ah-DaStar: You know . . . black lives matter and all that 🤷

JayceInURFace: That's stupid. I like Lila but making her Sleeping Beauty? I could see her as Lilac Fairy, maybe.

Rip-Ah-DaStar: A black Aurora is just weird. You think Madame will make her wear a blond wig? 😂

JaycelnURFace: IDK but my mom said Madame better make her take those braids out.

That had been three months ago. I motivated through 156 classes and 45 hours 30 minutes and 26 seconds of rehearsals without saying a word. Mommy said to let my dancing speak for me. And so far, my dancing said I was better than Jayce and Ripa.

Still, how could my friends talk mess about me like that?

Showtime

My costume squeezes me like a warm hug. I look exactly like one of those ballerinas frozen inside a snow globe, pink tights penciled under a flat platter tutu—a chocolate dream draped in pink and gold tulle. My braids are tucked neatly into a large bun with a tiny gold tiara nested on top. I look the part.

My heart pounds, pushing the oil my arms and legs need to obey the directions in my head—French words that my brain easily translates: pah duh shah, jet-tay, shuh-nay. They battle with the words from the group chat, fighting for control of my thoughts and my body.

Diversity pick.

Pas de chat.

Black lives matter . . . and all that.

Jeté. Jeté. Leap. Leap.

Better make her take those braids out.

Châiné. Châiné. Turn, turn, turn like a spinning top.

Black lives matter. Take those braids out. Black lives matter. Take those braids out.

Hate or dance, Lila.

Pick one.

A horn beckons and everyone except me goes onto the stage. It's time.

I close my eyes, inhale until my lungs are full. My body takes over, stamping out any doubt I ever had that I don't deserve this.

I step onto the stage, wave to the townspeople, and give Jayce an extra-long stare before I leap across, floating through the air like a feather someone blew off their hand.

It is my sixteenth birthday. I am a princess. The village has come to pay their respects. Strings pluck, first slowly then into a frenzy, signaling Princess Aurora is here.

I am here.

AMERICA DOESN'T LOVE US BACK BY FLOYD COOPER

TARGET BY PAT CUMMINGS

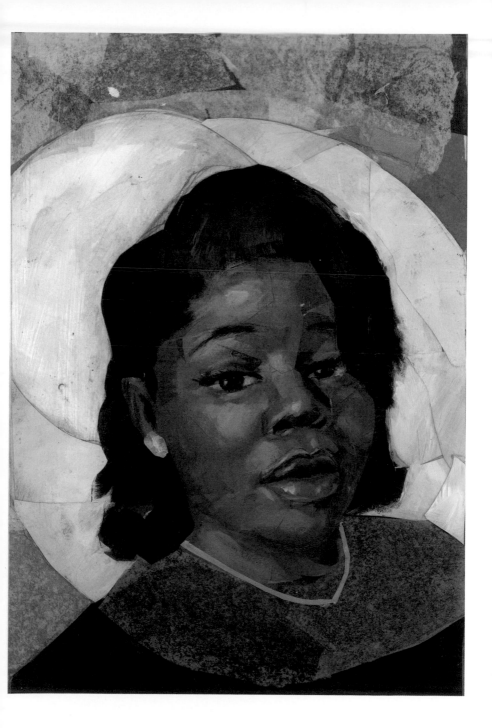

BREONNA TAYLOR, REMEMBER HER NAME! BY LONDON LADD

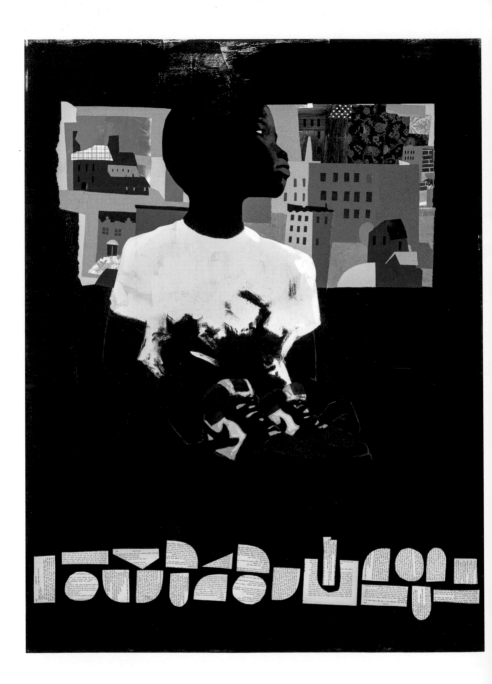

A BLACK BOY'S JOURNEY BY JAMES E. RANSOME

E PLURIBUS, II BY EKUA HOLMES

BROTHER'S MURDER, REMIX BY ERIC VELASQUEZ

GIVE ME FLOWERS BY SHANNON WRIGHT

EMPOWERED READER BY VANESSA BRANTLEY-NEWTON

THE TREATMENT OF THE CHILDREN HAD BEEN GETTING STEADILY WORSE FOR THE LAST TWO WEEKS IN THE FORM OF KICKING, SPITTING, AND GENERAL ABUSE.

In 1957, civil rights activist and journalist Daisy Bates wrote a letter to Roy Wilkins, then executive secretary of the National Association for the Advancement of Colored People that focused on the treatment of nine Black students who had recently integrated Central High School in Little Rock, Arkansas. Called the "Little Rock Nine," these young people were the first Black students to be enrolled at the school after the 1954 U.S. Supreme Court ruled segregated public schools unconstitutional. White citizens fought vigorously to keep the high school segregated. Arkansas governor Orval Faubus defied the U.S. court order to desegregate and even sent the Arkansas National Guard to Little Rock to prevent the Black students from entering the school. President Dwight Eisenhower was forced to send in federal troops to stop the violence and to enforce the law. The abuses against the students continued, however, once they were admitted, as Bates states in her letter.

THE TREATMENT OF THE LITTLE ROCK NINE

CENTRAL HIGH SCHOOL, 1957

DAISY BATES

Mr. Roy Wilkins
20 West 40th Street
New York, N.Y.

Dear Mr. Wilkins:

Conditions are yet pretty rough in the school for the children. Last week, Minnie Jean's mother, Mrs. W. B. Brown, asked me to go over to the school with her for a conference with the principal, and the two assistant principals. Subject of the conference: "Firmer disciplinary measures, and the withdrawal of Minnie Jean from the glee club's Christmas program." The principal had informed Minnie Jean in withdrawing her from the program that "When it is definitely decided that Negroes will go to school here with the whites, and the troops are removed, then you will be able to participate in all activities." We strongly challenged this statement, which he denied making in that fashion.

We also pointed out that the treatment of the children had been getting steadily worse for the last two weeks in the form of kicking, spitting, and general abuse. As a result of our visit, stronger measures are being taken against the white students who are guilty of committing these offenses. For instance, a boy who had been suspended for two weeks, flunked both six-weeks tests, and on his return to school, the first day he knocked Gloria Ray into her locker. As a result of our visit, he was given an indefinite suspension.

The superintendent of schools also requested a conference the same afternoon. Clarence and I went down and spent about two hours. Here, again we pointed out that a three-day suspension given Hugh Williams for a sneak attack perpetrated on one of the Negro boys which knocked him out, and required a doctor's attention, was not sufficient punishment. We also informed him that our investigation revealed that there were many pupils willing to help if given the opportunity, and that

President Eisenhower was very much concerned about the Little Rock crisis. He has stated his willingness to come down and address the student body if invited by student leaders of the school. This information was passed on to the principal of the school, but we have not been assured that leadership would be given to children in the school who are willing to organize for law and order. However, we have not abandoned the idea. Last Friday, the 13th, I was asked to call Washington and see if we could get FBI men placed in the school December 16-18.

Thanks for sending Clarence to help. I don't know how I would have made it without him. I am enclosing a financial statement, and as you can see, we are in pretty bad shape financially. On December 18, we will probably have to make bond for three of our officials from the North Little Rock Branch. December 18, midnight, is the deadline for filing names and addresses of members and contributors. I have talked with Mrs. Birdie Williams, and we are attempting to have them spend the night away from their homes, because we have been informed that they plan to arrest them after midnite.

I am suggesting that a revolving fund be set up here of $1,000.00 to take care of emergencies, and an accounting could be given at the end of each month. We are having trouble getting cost bonds executed on the North Little Rock suit. We had to put up $510.00 collateral plus three co-signers. We informed Bob Carter of our difficulty, and he asked Jack to see what could be done on that end. Please check with him.

I have not heard anything from the scholarship trust papers. We have deposited the money received for the scholarship. Mrs. A. L. Mothershed, 1313 Chester street, mother of one of the children, is serving as trustee.

I would appreciate hearing from you pertaining to the above mentioned matters at your earliest convenience.

I plan to attend the board meeting on January 6.

Sincerely,
Daisy Bates

DARNELLA FRAZIER: EYEWITNESS

Carole Boston Weatherford

00:09:29

Seventeen, with an evening off from her job
at the mall, Darnella Frazier was walking
to the store when she saw a handcuffed man
in the street overpowered by four cops.
Right then and there, the ancestors called her
to bear witness—not only to the horror at hand
but to centuries of terror against Black people.
Five feet away, Darnella turned her phone's lens
on George Floyd. Prone, with one cop's knee
on his neck and two cops oppressing his body,
he begged for mercy, for his dead momma, for air,
mouthing pleas like a mantra. "I can't breathe."
Darnella did not flinch in the badge's glare.
Fearing less for her own safety than she did
a cover-up if no one captured the brutal truth,
she stood her ground, steadied her camera,
and focused on her mission. Because Darnella
did not turn a blind eye, the whole world
saw the injustice. Now not a soul can erase
the evil or deny that Black Lives Matter.

ELAPSE   SLO-MO   VIDEO   PHOTO   SQU

MY STOMACH HURTS. MY NECK HURTS. EVERYTHING HURTS. THEY'RE GOING TO KILL ME.

MY STOMACH HURTS. EVERYTHING HURTS. THEY'RE GOING TO KILL ME.

MOMMA. MOMMA. I'M DEAD.—GEORGE FLOYD

HOW TO BE AN ACTIVIST

DON TATE

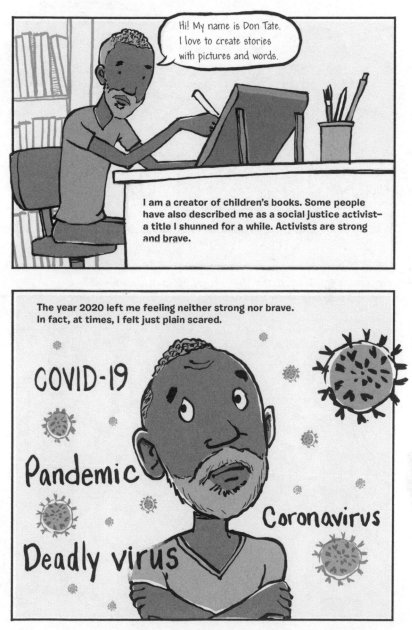

Hi! My name is Don Tate. I love to create stories with pictures and words.

I am a creator of children's books. Some people have also described me as a social justice activist—a title I shunned for a while. Activists are strong and brave.

The year 2020 left me feeling neither strong nor brave. In fact, at times, I felt just plain scared.

COVID-19

Pandemic

Coronavirus

Deadly virus

When the pandemic first hit, my wife stopped working at her office—she worked from home with me. She used Zoom to communicate with her coworkers. It was confusing sometimes.

Soon, our son, a student at the University of Texas, came home, too. His classes were now online.

But with each passing day, the news got darker. A lot of people were dying from COVID-19—especially Black and Brown people. Jobs and homes were lost. Our leaders didn't seem to care.

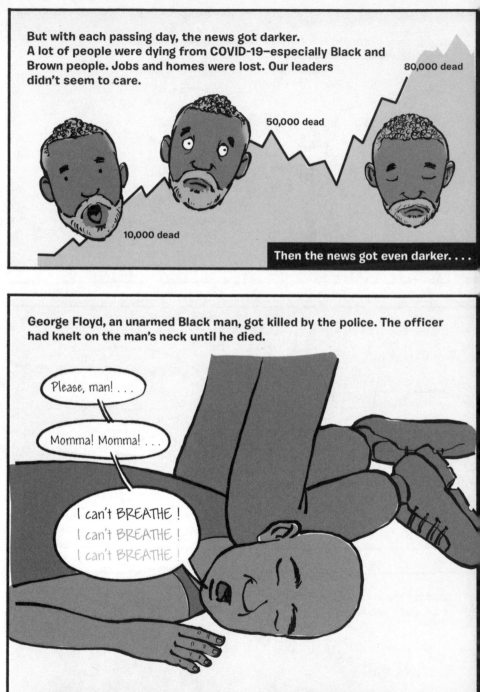

80,000 dead

50,000 dead

10,000 dead

Then the news got even darker. . . .

George Floyd, an unarmed Black man, got killed by the police. The officer had knelt on the man's neck until he died.

Please, man! . . .

Momma! Momma! . . .

I can't BREATHE!
I can't BREATHE!
I can't BREATHE!

I couldn't stand to watch as the man begged for his life. I cried when he called out to his momma. No one deserved to be treated that way, especially by those who are supposed to serve and protect.

Two months before, in Louisville, Kentucky, a young woman, Breonna Taylor, had been killed by police who raided her home—searching for someone else.

Ahmaud Arbery

Breonna Taylor

Before that, there was the killing of Ahmaud Arbery in Brunswick, Georgia. He was unarmed when he was shot by a former police officer and his son. He was simply out jogging.

I began to worry about my own family. Could something like this happen to my wife or son, too? Might I get killed by the police? Or a virus? As a Black man living in America, I didn't feel safe anywhere—inside or outside of my home.

Protests broke out in Minneapolis over George Floyd's death. Then the protests branched out all over the world. Even friends here in Austin—Black and white—marched. I felt emotional reading their tweets.

NO JUSTICE NO PEACE #BLM

BLACK LIVES MATTER

BLACK LIVES

My wife and son were doing their part. I searched for a way to do mine. My book projects required a lot of research. I was learning about so many people of all races who used their individual talents to fight against racism— to be anti-racist, to make the world a better place.

I realized that my children's book work serves the same purpose. I write stories for children about inspirational Black people. My stories demonstrate Black brilliance, resilience, creativity, talent, and love.

MY HERO IS A BLACK COWBOY

ROBERT H. MILLER

I was eleven years old, when my mom and dad bought a television set. It changed how I spent my time. However, on each Saturday evening, my brother and five of our buddies would walk to the neighborhood movie theater. Action movies were generally Westerns, and I couldn't wait to get a ticket so all of us could pile into the back row. The back row was our little haven. There we could act out during the film, unseen.

Westerns had a particular impact on me when I was growing up, whether watching them in the theater or on television. I identified so much with the white cowboy hero, I became him. It never occurred to me there were no African Americans in those films. I saw myself as the star, not even aware that the hero didn't look like me. On rare occasions you would see an African

American actor, but his role was no more than comic relief. He would carry around an iron skillet, for example, but never wore a holster with a gun. Those episodes provided laughter for the predominately white audience, while I, embarrassed, slumped further down in my seat, too ashamed to look at the screen. The Black actor was eventually killed off, and I was relieved. Looking back, I know the impact that had on me as a Black kid. I never thought that I could be a Black hero. I was held hostage to another culture's history, trying to make it my own, as if Black culture had no heroes.

One afternoon my uncle asked my mother if he could take my brother and me to a rodeo. She agreed, and I was ecstatic. My uncle had purchased our tickets beforehand, so we walked right in and got great seats near the front row. I had watched rodeos on television and in the movies, but this was the first time I got up close and personal to real cowboys. The arena was full and there was a feeling of excitement in the air. After welcoming everybody, the master of ceremonies announced the contestants. The music was loud country western songs. The smell of the sawdust and animals filled my nostrils and helped to pique my curiosity.

After watching the earlier acts, it was time for bull riding, the event everyone wanted to see. The MC gave a little background story on each contestant, then waved his hand. The gate flew open. Out sprang the first bull and rider. I had no idea how big bulls were in real life, but this bull looked to be the size of a truck! Okay, maybe not that big, but you get the idea. He wasn't small.

The first contestant didn't last three seconds before being thrown high into the air, landing on the ground in the arena. Contestant after contestant was thrown by the bulls. Since bull riding was the last event, people began to gather their things to leave. My uncle signaled my brother and me to pack up. But in the middle of following his suggestion, something happened.

The MC hurried back to the loudspeaker and announced that there was a late entry. Everyone should take a seat. I looked toward the gate as it opened. A cowboy dressed in black with a short cigar in his mouth sat atop the bucking bull. He was an African American. My heart sank to my knees. I thought I would be embarrassed again. This time there was no place to hide. The arena was quiet as the Black cowboy still sat on this bull's back. The bull couldn't throw him. No matter how high the bull jumped in the air, twisted and bucked, this Black cowboy had him figured out. What amazed me the most was that the cowboy's cigar was still in his mouth. A buzzer ended the ride. The audience cheered and clapped.

"I've never seen anyone stay on that bull," I heard one man say.

When the Black cowboy jumped off the bull's back,

the rodeo clowns ran out to distract the bull. The Black cowboy lifted his right hand into the air and made a fist, the winner of the bull-riding contest!

I learned a lesson that day—someone like me could be a cowboy hero.

Shortly after our trip to the rodeo, my mother revealed to me that my great-uncles were real cowboys who lived and worked in Texas and Mexico. But as a kid growing up in Oregon, I didn't know about my great-uncles' history. My schools didn't teach us about Black heroes of the West, either.

I wrote the Reflections of a Black Cowboy series for young readers to tell the African American side of the Old West. I realized that young Black kids, *all* kids, need to know that history—about the Buffalo soldiers, Nat Love, Mary Fields, Bass Reeves, and other Black heroes of the West.

Black youngsters need heroes to identify with, like those Black pioneers and cowboys who helped to settle the American West. When you know your history, you can be free to see yourself as a hero.

When Black lives matter, Black heroes matter, too.

Adios, amigos, giddyup!

DRUMBEAT, RING SHOUT, ROLL CALL, CYPHER*

IBI ZOBOI

Imagine, child—
You are rhythm.
It's not just the way you dance or
bop your head to a beat, or drop a rhyme.
It's the way that you are with movement and flow
like planets rotating around the sun
    in perfect time, divine.

Listen, child—
The power to hold a drum within your body.
Like the sound of your ancestors' feet on dirt
    ground
shuffling round and round, summoning something
    new,
maybe it's you rising out of the bass to become
    blues, gospel, jazz, and hip-hop.

Imagine, child—
You are a conjuring of the future
within a ring game of your
great-grandmothers and -grandfathers,
hand in hand to form a belly
out of which you are born.
Don't you know you are their
*   song for freedom?*

Listen, child—
As they call your name
one by one, two by two.
You step forward and answer the call
with your dance moves and poetry,
your science and extraterrestrial technology.
You make yourself a new world,
stepping into your purpose, soaring into your
*   dream*
*   to fly, and fly, and fly.*

Imagine, child—
you are an angel made of stardust
riding high in the sky
taking up space like astronauts.
And with your brothers and sisters
beside you, hand in hand like your ancestors,
you form this cypher around the earth

*like Saturn's rings, you hold everything within
your
deep, deep brown skin.*

*Listen, child—
You are your grandmothers' song,
your mother's prayer,
your father's dream.*

*Imagine, child—
You are the drumbeat and the ring shout.
You are the roll call and the cypher.**

*The **drum** is a musical instrument that is present
throughout all cultures in Africa and the African diaspora.
During slavery in the United States, the drum was
prohibited because it was believed that enslaved Africans
used it to send messages. However, they used their bodies
and other instruments to make music during celebrations,
one of which was the ring shout, a circle dance where music
is made by stomping and shuffling the feet and clapping to
a call-and-response. A roll call is when someone calls out
names for attendance. A **cypher** in hip-hop is a gathering
of rappers and break-dancers who share their skills with a
crowd of onlookers.

DERAY MCKESSON

DeRay Mckesson is a civil rights activist focused primarily on issues of innovation, equity, and justice. As a leading voice in the Black Lives Matter movement and a cofounder of Campaign Zero, DeRay has worked to connect individuals with knowledge and tools to help create a more just society and provide citizens and policy makers with commonsense policies that ensure equity. He is a former schoolteacher.

Wade Hudson & Cheryl Willis Hudson: How did you become a leader in the social justice movement in this country?

DeRay Mckesson: Teaching changed my life—it is what made me most clearly understand systemic racism, that inequity and poverty are by design and that we not only deserve so much more but that justice is possible. When Mike Brown was killed in Ferguson, Missouri, I felt called to go stand in solidarity. I'd planned to go for two days, but on the second day I was tear-gassed and that changed my life. We hadn't done anything wrong—the police had killed someone, not us. And yet, I was running for my life. I vowed that night to fight to make sure that this never happened to another person. It was that night that I committed to the work of ending police violence.

WH & CWH: What was it like for a Black youngster like you growing up in Baltimore?

DM: Both of my parents were once addicted to drugs. My mother left when I was three; my father raised us. In so many ways, I grew up in a community of recovery—seeing people in their hardest moments work to put their lives back together and that has always stuck with me. I grew up seeing the power of community to change lives, to change the world. I saw the power of relationships to help people find their power, saw the power and limits of love. Baltimore taught me that love is often not enough—that love is powerful and that there are often larger things at play that shape the choices that people can make. It's our responsibility to make sure that systems allow people to make the best choices for themselves and that we make all of the resources available to make that happen. Baltimore taught me how much we deserve. And Baltimore also taught me that joy is a part of our work. We did not have much money as kids and we always had joy. We always knew love. We always had community. Money did not define our sense of joy.

WH & CWH: What does the phrase *Black Lives Matter* mean to you?

DM: It is both an affirmation and a belief that we are bringing into practice.

WH & CWH: As a former teacher, how would you help your students understand the importance of Black Lives Matter and the social justice movement.

DM: I would teach my students the truth about our history. I only learned surface issues about systemic racism and injustice in school—it was always taught as history, as the past. It was never taught as present. I would help my students understand that the history is present, that systemic racism is by design, and that they have power. I never learned that in school. I tried to teach it, even as a math teacher. Our students deserve the truth.

I would teach my students that the movement is theirs, too. The movement is people coming together to fight for change. Movements are born from the belief that we can make this world into the world that we deserve for it to be.

WH & CWH: How can those who are not Black fight against racism and help promote justice and equality for all?

DM: We need accomplices who are willing to stand in the fire with us, or even stand in the fire on our behalf. People expect me to talk about injustice because I'm directly impacted. They don't expect people who aren't directly impacted to be advocates. We need white people who are not the victims of systemic racism to speak out even more forcefully than we do. We need them to step up alongside us. We need them to sacrifice their comfort because it's the right thing to do. We need white people to fight.

WH & CWH: Are you hopeful about the future? Why or why not?

DM: I have never been more confident that it is possible to dismantle this system and build a new one in my lifetime. And I have never been more worried that we might not get there. Time will tell whether we can do it or not.

We have a set of tools that simply didn't exist before. We have a chance to build on the legacy of those who came before us and to finally do the things that they imagined. The police are the only institution that we fight in civil rights that has gotten more power over time, not less. I can see the end, clearly. I can see a path there. But it will take all of us. And the forces against us—those on the right, the white supremacists—they are organized and loud and use the nostalgia of racism to dull our work sometimes. But yes, I'm hopeful. I know another world is possible and that we will have to fight to birth her. She's coming.

FOR I AM MY MOTHER'S DAUGHTER, AND THE DRUMS OF AFRICA STILL BEAT IN MY HEART. THEY WILL NOT LET ME REST WHILE THERE IS A SINGLE NEGRO BOY OR GIRL WITHOUT A CHANCE TO PROVE HIS WORTH.

MARY MCLEOD BETHUNE'S "LAST WILL AND TESTAMENT"

CHERYL WILLIS HUDSON AND WADE HUDSON

What could she leave to inspire and encourage the people whom she loved so much and for whom she had dedicated most of her life to serve? Dr. Mary McLeod Bethune pondered this question as she neared the end of her extraordinary life.

The fifteenth of seventeen children, Bethune was born in 1875, ten years after the Civil War ended. Formerly enslaved, her parents had saved enough money to buy their own small parcel of land to farm near Mayesville, South Carolina.

The only member of her family to attend school, a determined Bethune walked five miles to get to the one-room building. When she came home, she taught her family what she had learned. She also helped to cultivate crops on her family's farm.

From this humble beginning, Mary McLeod Bethune went on to become one of the most important national leaders of her time. She advocated for issues such as civil rights, women's rights, education, and health care, and was appointed to numerous commissions by those who sought her counsel.

In 1904, with only a few dollars in her pocket, Bethune rented a house and started a school for Black children. She spent decades growing her school, raising money to construct buildings and to buy school supplies and materials for her students and teachers. Her school later merged with the Cookman Institute and became Bethune-Cookman College, educating thousands of Black students.

Now retired, she sat in her residence on the Bethune-Cookman campus, thinking about what she could leave as a legacy to inspire her people. She decided to write a will, calling it her "Last Will & Testament." The items that Bethune listed did not include money, stocks, or bonds. She did not include property or material possessions that are passed on traditionally to family members or heirs through a legally binding document. Her Last Will & Testament was a list of principles and values that had guided her life. *Ebony* magazine published it in August 1955, several months after she died.

She began with the words "I leave you . . ."

Love was first. She saw it as the highest principle.

For her, love was interracial, interreligious, and international.

Hope was a principle that would guide Black people's political and economic progress for the future despite the past degradation of slavery.

The challenge of developing confidence in one another was key to cooperative economics and mutual aid. She emphasized building Black institutions such as banks, insurance companies, and other businesses.

A thirst for education was paramount and essential for young people to pursue opportunities for advancement in all areas of human endeavor.

A respect for the uses of power should be intelligently directed to maintain our democracy and to achieve social justice and freedom for all humankind.

Faith was a major principle in a life devoted to service. She wrote that without faith, nothing was possible, and with it, nothing was impossible.

Racial dignity was a must. Bethune was proud that Black people had made many contributions to the world of which they should be proud. She wrote that she would not exchange her color for all the wealth in the world.

A desire to live harmoniously with your fellow men was based on the Golden Rule. Recognizing common problems among people was essential for unity, brotherhood, and international peace.

Responsibility to our young people was crucial because Bethune was convinced that they had enormous potential. "Our children must never lose their zeal for building a better world," she wrote.

Although it was published more than six decades ago, the principles in Dr. Mary McLeod Bethune's "Last Will & Testament" still speak to us today as our society grapples with issues of systemic racism, social injustice, and inequality.

CLAIMING MY SPACE

Adedayo Perkovich

So sit on what once could've been a steeple
There is so much we aren't seeing.

My mother signed me up for a tour of Central Park. City kid that I am, I was pretty confident I knew all that needed to be known about the quintessential New York City park. Hours trudging through the place I'd been playing in forever? No thanks. But touring the park a few weeks later, I found a hidden world I'd missed. We stopped at a clearing of nondescript grass, surrounding a tree with particularly twisted branches. Our guide spoke: "This site is a part of Seneca Village." He shared the history of a vibrant, multicultural nineteenth-century community that included hundreds of African American property owners with voting rights, who had built schools, homes, and churches. Children like me had played here, at a time when most of their peers in the United States were enslaved. This beautiful and complicated history was demolished to make way for the expanse of nature I loved. *Why hadn't I known?*

I took in the scenery I was so quick to dismiss as a normal part of the park. There were no signs, nothing to distinguish this place. My eyes fell on the cobblestones our tour guide pointed out as remnants of village buildings. But I came back to the tree, following the uniquely distorted paths of its branches. Beams of sunlight shone gently through the leaves. I stood there, trying to reconcile my appreciation for the natural beauty of the park with the destruction employed to create it. The community of people like me, literally demolished to make space for the nature where I felt so at home—that I considered to be a part of my city experience. And then came an even more troubling thought: *How would I have known?*

A month later, summer break had ended and a high school workload gave me no free time for park tours and staring at trees. But even though I couldn't return to Seneca Village, I encountered a different set of intellectual challenges. I felt isolated and traumatized after reading in class about the physical and mental abuse Black people have and continue to experience in this country. On my bus rides to and from school, I would watch Central Park speed by and ask myself, *Are you doing enough? Do your efforts to educate really matter? Every time you push yourself to speak up in class, share a poem or write an article, attend a protest with peers— did it make an impact?* Frustrated, I watched the trees pass.

Fast-forward to 3:00 a.m. on my sixteenth birthday. I sat on my rug instead of sleeping before the long flight ahead of me. With all my belongings packed, there was nothing left to do but worry. This school trip to Ghana was an opportunity to learn more about African history! But I was nervous. I *knew* I would make a mistake; I'd prove I wasn't African enough, didn't live up to my Nigerian name and family. These thoughts stayed with me in the car to JFK, and I tried to push them aside as I chatted with friends at the airport. We waved goodbye to our parents and took flight. I spent fourteen hours listening to music and curating playlists to calm my nerves; we landed as I turned up my Afrobeats playlist for confidence. Still, our group of Black Americans flustered by travel paperwork felt conspicuous at the Accra International Airport.

When I found out that our first destination in Ghana was Assin Manso, the Ancestral Slave River Park, I wanted to run back to my room. "The Ancestors" have been a part of my life for a long time, in childhood folktales and museums, in and outside of school. I'd never felt my connection to them click. But when we started walking down to the river where captured Africans would take their last bath, I felt a shift. We took off our shoes to walk as those enslaved people had over this rough, sacred ground. My feet were so soft; they were new to this kind of pressure. I worried they were not yet resilient enough for the journey. I found myself near tears imagining being led down this beautiful tree-lined path to the ugliness I knew my ancestors endured. We came to two arches, one marked *Door of No Return* and the other *Door of Return*. The Ancestors could not return, so we recognized and remembered their stories by walking through the Door of Return, completing their journey home. Even though they were taken from their home, they, like the Seneca Village community, created their own spaces, and their strength made my present possible.

After returning from Ghana, I spent my first few months reflecting on the experience. Even with my heavy backpack I walked taller, feeling more confident in my grasp of my cultural history, laughed loudly and freely in hallways sharing memories of the trip with new friends, and connected with the humanity of the African peoples we learned about in humanities classes. Filled with pride, respect, sadness, and joy, I felt like a stronger, fuller intellectual and emotional version of myself. And it was after these months of reflection that I was asked to write poetry for a public art project in Central Park. I chose to write about Seneca Village.

I can hear my poem now, right there in the park.

I felt the imprint my shoe made in this softer place

After a year of working to understand, accept, and appreciate the ways in which *I* approach social justice work, and helping other kids of color do the same, I think back to my trips to Ghana and Seneca Village. I stand in Central Park, surrounded by the trees I love, by the sign that tells visitors of an AME church that once was, with words from my poem ringing in my ears. A peace comes over me as I look around, recognizing the existence, beauty, and importance of Black communities before me, and the creativity and change stemming from the life and humanity of Black kids like me everywhere. I feel heard, and in the light breeze, I feel the presence and strength of the people whose lives I honor.

Existing in our communities as our authentic selves is an act of resistance, a mechanism for social change. The space I take up as a poet, an amateur painter, a Meklit, Khalid, Chloe x Halle, Harry Styles, and Sheku Kanneh-Mason fan, and clumsy *Avatar: The Last Airbender* superfan, carrying all of my burdens and bright spots, has value. I honor my ancestors by claiming my space.

FREEDOM IN THE MUSIC

Curtis Hudson

I always loved to play the guitar. I heard it being played all the time when I was growing up. My father strummed it. My uncles and neighbors gathered on front porches and played blues on Saturday nights while women fried tasty fish back in their kitchens. Outside our homes, we had our own Black nightclubs and places where we could perform. Music was part of our day-to-day. When popular Black entertainers like Sam Cooke, Louis Armstrong, Nat King Cole, Ella Fitzgerald, and James Brown were featured on television shows, we watched them intently. They were special. To me, their music seemed to erase that color line that separated people in our everyday lives. Seeing these entertainers on television made aspiring, young Black musicians like me feel proud and special.

We could matter. Perhaps one day we, too, could share what we had to offer to the world.

So, my brother Wilbert, who played bass guitar, and I practiced long hours, learning the latest R & B and pop songs by ear. It was during this time that I found myself, found my purpose. Just having that guitar in my hands made me feel that I mattered.

I discovered the potential music has to bring people of different races together when I was a teenager. By the ages of fifteen and fourteen, my brother and I had learned to play our instruments well enough to join a local band called Joe Hunt and the SS Malibus. Our small-town audiences were totally Black in Mansfield, Louisiana, and very typical of other segregated places in the South of the 1960s. But one day, our band was invited to play for a prom at the local all-white high school. This was a first and a big deal. Up to that time, I had few interactions with white kids. Black kids remained in our own communities and the white kids stayed in theirs. That's what racial segregation meant.

The white kids loved the Malibus' funky, danceable music. While the band played, our lead singer, Roy C. Hunt, did all the latest dances—the Jerk, the Mashed Potato, the Hitch Hike, the Pony. The white kids gathered around him trying to pick up the moves. Roy C. was a great James Brown imitator and they loved that, responding as if Roy was the real James Brown. The

Malibus jammed and they danced and partied. They cheered us on and told us how great we sounded.

"Play that guitar!" one girl shouted to me as I performed a solo.

"Y'all sound like the record," a skinny boy said, clapping his hands to the rhythm.

For those few hours it didn't matter that we were Black. For those white teenagers, it was all about the music, the dancing, and the excitement of prom night. We were all just teenagers doing what teenagers do.

But later in the week, on the streets downtown, when we passed those same kids who had attended the prom, they wouldn't even speak to us. We knew not to speak to them. Things were back to business as usual. We mattered while we entertained them, but afterward we didn't. For a few hours that night, color did not define us.

What remained constant with me was whenever I had my guitar, rehearsing or playing onstage, I was somebody special, not just another Colored boy ignored and devalued in a segregated town in the South. I mattered even if some people thought I didn't.

One day, a local white appliance store owner who had seen us perform invited our band to his store to record some of our songs. He told us he thought we were talented enough to make a record demo. He wasn't the typical Southern white we often encountered, and he and his family treated us with respect. The band spent the evening recording R & B tunes on his recording equipment. We felt like professional musicians. Because of that experience, I knew I would become a professional recording artist—writing my own songs and playing my own music.

When I grew older, I learned about the struggles of those Black entertainers we used to follow on television. Despite their outward success, they still "didn't matter" and were not valued like Frank Sinatra, Dean Martin, the Beatles, the Rolling Stones, or even lesser known white artists.

Still, I continued to play guitar and write songs. My music became a path to my own personal freedom. It has taken me places that a young Black boy in Mansfield couldn't have dreamed of. I have written hit songs for artists such as Madonna, Missy Elliott, and John Legend. And I have passed my love for music on to my son, Eric. He, too, has established a successful career in music, working with Kanye West, Mariah Carey, Justin Timberlake, and others. Yet, he still faces questions about his value and importance in the music industry. Maybe not as much as I did, but he still must demand that he matters, that his Black life matters at all times, just as I have had to do and still must do.

BACK TO MYSELF

TIFFANY JEWELL

The summer before I started kindergarten, my dad got into a car accident. He was in a coma for what felt like too long, and when he woke up, he had lost his memory—his memories stayed somewhere else. And then his mom (my grandma) moved her family south, taking my dad with her. My sister and I stayed north. Our connection with my father's family was through phone lines and then not at all.

As the years passed, I lost connection to the Black side of my heritage. I couldn't remember the color of my grandaddy's car or the comic books my dad kept in the white cabinet in his apartment. The smell of alcohol from the liquor store my grandmother owned never came back to me. The memories of sitting alongside my sister, listening to one of our favorites—Tina

Turner's "What's Love Got to Do with It"—on the grass next to Daddy's car turned into old stories without meaning. Those memories that could have kept me connected to my father's family, *my* Blackness, continued to fade.

But the memories I collected with my mother's family, the white side of my heritage—afternoon tea, reading *The Secret Garden,* and summertime picnics in the park—kept building and growing.

I used to wonder if I was Black enough, if my loose curls and my light brown skin were enough proof to the world that I was truly Black. But the world kept trying to tell me otherwise. Those were the years in which I lost myself trying to figure out who I was. I didn't know who I could be. They were years spent burning my scalp to straighten my hair, hanging out at the mall, having crushes on white boys, and always trying to prove that I belonged to a world that wasn't ready for me. I was the girl with the ambiguously light skin tone, freckles across my face (a gift from my dad), the brown almond eyes (another gift from my dad), and the hair that resisted no matter how hard I tried to control my curls. I moved through a maze of whiteness, trying to find meaning within myself.

Then I connected with my Black sister-friends. They came with different names at different times in my life. We met in different places during assemblies and gatherings and stayed connected through social media and Zoom meetings. We found each other in spaces that didn't want us to find our whole selves, and they always met me with arms stretched wide for an embrace and a welcoming. They—the many of them—were always there and helped me rediscover my true self.

They reflected my wholeness, everything that made me who I am, back to me and reminded me of *our* common humanity.

My past experiences had me believing I was not worthy of being a full human. I was called "mulatto" and was often asked to choose which of my heritages to embrace. I was seldom allowed to be a whole person, always half one or half the other.

With every smile, and laugh, and embrace my sister-friends offered, they brought back memories of old experiences of my youth, with my dad's family and other friends, and presented me with the love and strength of a new beginning. My sister-friends brought back the memories. And the memories brought me back to my old self.

My new sister-friends, even when we find ourselves tired from work, dance to songs that fall off our tongues as if we own them. We release our joy.

A couple of years ago, one of my new sister-friends and I found ourselves rushing through the cold in a new city. Laughing our way through the freezing temperatures, she reminded me of when I was three years old and playing in the snow outside my trailer-sized preschool classroom. The memory was of my old friend, my old sis. We had cleared a pathway for all our friends with child-sized shovels and I slipped on the ice and hit my mouth and she picked me right up. Without hesitation, her arms wrapped around me and brought me to warmth and safety. She was a year older than me, taller, stronger, more self-assured. I still remember that moment when she showed me how to be caring and brave and strong.

I am transported back in time to the octagonal table in my grade-school cafeteria, our lunch boxes open, and I am with my best friend, my sister-friend. Every day, the lyrics of songs we hear on the radio fill our voices; we shake our shoulders and pretend we are the ones performing those Top 40 hits. We are filled with belly laughs and love. She is the one I seek out every day; she is mine and I am hers. We are the ones we each pick first whenever partners have to be chosen.

I still hum "The Locomotion" and remember how free we could be in ourselves; she showed me how to make moments of joy happen every day because they can.

After years of not knowing that I could be me—a whole Black biracial person—I know who I am. I carry all the old friendships and experiences with my Black sister-friends and my dad's people with me, wherever I go. And all the new friendships I've made, and will make, come along, too. My sister-friends have always reflected beauty, love, strength, resistance, and joy back to me. And, because of them, I am now whole.

RECOGNIZE!

CHERYL WILLIS HUDSON

Ayanna took a deep breath, then exhaled slowly as she shifted her weight from her left leg to her right. She was standing in the middle of the basketball court at the community center, right next to her best friend, Kelly. Fifty other kids dressed in shorts and yellow T-shirts surrounded them. Everyone was having fun singing, dancing, and doing cheers and chants. Harambee was always a fun time to start summer days at Freedom School.

Harambee meant "Let's pull together," and for thirty whole minutes it helped to set the tone for the rest of the day. The college students who had been se-lected to be servant leaders for the Freedom School led kids like Ayanna and Kelly, who were called "scholars" during a day of programs and activities. By providing a supportive environment, Freedom School encouraged the scholars to excel and believe in their ability to make a difference in themselves and in their families, schools, communities, country, and world.

This was Ayanna's first year attending Freedom School. She couldn't wait for Harambee to start each new day. It always began with Read Aloud, when adults from the community came to share stories. Then they all sang Freedom School's motivational theme song, "Something Inside So Strong." The words actually made Ayanna feel strong and powerful. Recognition time followed and everyone knew they would all have a chance to shine.

"Take a seat, take a seat. Take a load off your feet! Take a seat, take a seat. Take a load off your feet!" shouted one of the servant leaders.

They all got quiet and sat down. Then Ayanna stood up. The circle painted on the gym floor made her feel like she was standing on a stage with a spotlight shining on her. Normally very quiet, she felt a little flutter in her chest as she stood uncomfortably facing the group.

But today Ayanna was excited. She had been practicing for hours for this moment so she could speak.

She cupped her right hand around the contours of her mouth and spoke in a clear voice just like she had practiced.

"I have a recognition."

Most of the time, she spoke very softly while staring at her feet. So she was surprised by how far her voice carried in the gym.

The other scholars answered back as they had been taught to do.

"Recognize!"

"I said, I have a recognition," Ayanna repeated with confidence in an even louder voice.

"Recognize!" was the group's response. The second time they were louder, too.

Ayanna took another deep breath and smiled broadly.

"I'd like to recognize Kelly, who is my best friend. Today is her tenth birthday. I want to recognize Kelly because she knows how to be a BFF. She volunteered to share her birthday celebration with me today even though my birthday is two days away."

"Recognize!" the scholars shouted. Then they sang Stevie Wonder's version of "Happy Birthday."

"Happy birthday to you. Happy birthday to you! Happy birthday!"

Ayanna and Kelly stood tall, high-fived each other, and then took their seats. Ayanna had recognized her friend's good deed but had also gotten some shine of her own. Standing before a large group was a big step for her. It was a step that made the Freedom School staff, servant leaders, and scholars happy to see her growth.

Torrey stood up next. "I have a recognition," he called out. A tall, lanky twelve-year-old, Torrey rapped to anyone who would listen. He loved writing poems and made up rhymes all the time.

"Recognize!" the scholars responded.

"I said I have a recognition!" repeated Torrey. He emphasized the "I" and pointed to his chest with his thumb in a rhythmic deejay motion.

"Recognize!!" the group answered.

"I want to recognize our servant leaders for all their hard work in bringing community leaders to Freedom School," Torrey said in a loud, clear voice. "They share Read Alouds with us. Now check this out."

My name is Torrey and rapping is my story.
I made this rhyme so servant leaders can shine.
Grab a book. Take a look. And see how we cook.
I got it. You got it. Now everyone enjoy it!

"Good job! Good job! G-double O-D J-O-B! Good job! Good job!" the scholars sang out.

Ayanna and Kelly looked up at Torrey, hugged each other again, and smiled at their friends. Harambee was such a good time of the day. Recognition always gave everyone a chance to say something positive about someone else. Not only could they acknowledge special events like a birthday, but Recognition was a time to share shine with others who showed leadership, good work, or acts of kindness. Ayanna was glad that being recognized wasn't about wearing new clothes or having a cute haircut or getting a fresh pair of sneakers. It wasn't about material things.

Today it was Ayanna's, Torrey's, and Kelly's turn to Recognize. Tomorrow, others would have their opportunity—maybe a servant leader, a parent, or someone from the community.

Harambee had ended, and the scholars were ready to move on to more reading activities on the Freedom School schedule. Learning how to be a good leader was important. And it was fun, too. Fun to recognize and to be recognized!

Recognize!

THE DEVIL IN THE FLOWERS

Homage to Virginia Hamilton: Master Storyteller

ALICIA D. WILLIAMS

As Black Americans proudly proclaim our identities, and that, yes, our lives matter, Virginia Hamilton's work serves as a reminder of our journey. Her stories, often referred to as "liberation literature," allow us to celebrate our past as we forge ahead fighting social injustices for a better future. We honor Ms. Hamilton for her literary contributions. And let us remember her words: "The books from which [children] learn must reflect movement and change and all of the infinite possibilities of minds at liberty."

A sea of yellow flowers faced Brianna. She wanted to run through them, making it part like Moses did the Red Sea. Run straight to Mother Hamilton's porch swing. But naw, she couldn't, on account of her mama fussing to stay put. Stay put she did, in the rocking chair, wondering what tale she was gon' miss today.

What if it's the one about people flying?

See, Mother Hamilton spun tales that would've

made both Grimm brothers shake in their socks. Ones about cats big as timber wolves, wicked Jack tricking the devil, and that horrible Hairy Man gobbling up little kids. Good ones! Scary ones! She had to go! Even the flower petals beckoned her.

Brianna crept—*shh*—down the steps of her porch. Soon as her toes touched the bottom, the screen door creaked open.

"Whatcha doing?" asked Mama.

"Nothing," said Brianna with antsy feet.

"Mmhmm," grunted Mama. "Look atcha, itchin' to scramble up that road."

Mama was right, 'cause as fast as her flip-flops patted back to the kitchen, Brianna took off. Her sundress slapped at her knees, spanking her for being disobedient. Brianna laughed and danced through the field, picking a bundle of flowers. She passed woods full of tall willows, singing insects, and croaking frogs.

Rrr-Rrr-Rrr. Brianna swore she heard the howls of cats from those folktales. She peered into the woods, seeing nothing but waving grass.

Rrr—Rrr—Rrr. There was the sound again, like a lion, creeping up.

She was so close to Mother Hamilton's.

Rrr—Rrr—Rrr.

A red truck pulled alongside her. Inside was a leathery faced man with frown lines deep as dried dirt. His nose was pointy and his hair greasy. "Hello, little girl. Know who I am?" His voice was scratchy, too.

He seemed familiar. But not from the market or church, nor school. *Where?* she thought, now wishing she'd stayed put like Mama warned.

"Some call me Mister Devil." His lips spread to a crooked smile, baring crooked yellow teeth.

Mister Devil? From the tale "Jack and the Devil"? But Mother Hamilton's stories weren't real, were they? Brianna could smell his moldy musk. Oh yes, *he* was real.

"Let's take a ride," he said, opening the door.

"Can't . . . got some place to be." Brianna quickly recalled that Jack was mean to his wife and kids, and the devil came to collect him. But Jack was a conniver and convinced the devil to fetch some apples from the apple tree.

"I'll take you," said Mister Devil, climbing out.

"But . . . you a stranger." Brianna stepped backward, recollecting how Jack then got out his pocket-knife.

"Don't be afraid," he said, grinning.

Brianna remembered! *He can't cross crosses.* With the devil up the tree, Jack cut crosses in the bark. And the devil was stuck! "What you bothering me for? I ain't don' nothing bad," she asked, stalling. Brianna slyly dropped two flowers onto the ground in the

139

shape of a T. She stepped to the left and dropped two more.

"Oh, the missus'll love you. You can take her some of them pretty flowers." His greedy beady eyes followed her. Eyes too greedy to notice.

"I'm just a kid." Drop-drop. Step.

"And I'm a friend to children."

Drop-drop. Step.

"Now you be still, so I can grab you."

"No, sir, can't let you do that." Drop-drop. Step. "Gotta get to Mother Hamilton's. She has stories I need to hear . . . for protection."

"Protection? Ha!" The devil laughed a big laugh. "No sucha thing!"

Brianna came full circle, facing him again. "If it wasn't for her stories, I wouldn't've been able to trap you . . . like Jack had."

At Jack's name, the devil gnashed his teeth. Jack: the only one who got away. He lunged for Brianna but fell backward. The devil looked about him. Circling all around were the flowers. "Crosses! No . . . please let me free!" he begged.

"Uh-uh. You'll just come back." Brianna turned to go.

"Ya can't leave me here!" cried the devil.

'Cause of Jack, Brianna knew the devil kept his word. "Promise you'll leave children alone forever, then I'll free you." He agreed.

Mister Devil cussed and cried as he fled away fast.

Brianna had faced the devil. Still, she skipped up that road because, shucks, Mother Hamilton's stories were more than scary tales, magical folklore, and stories of the past. . . . Mother Hamilton's folktales were beacons of light, hope, and wisdom. And we all need to hear them.

YOUR BREATH IS A SONG

Mahogany L. Browne

What does joy sound like
After you have stood up
Against the storm?
After your opinion becomes
its own thunder?
After your strong voice
lifts the sky?

What does the air feel like
After the people surround the city block
After the people's demands are finally met
After the city servants respond
With the high standard
Of their duty
To care for every citizen

All the country's people
Move in rhythm regardless of our different paths
All the country's citizens celebrate
An orchestra rejoiced

Because no one can tell you that the growing
Echo in your chest ain't a song
Your breath is a song

Wherever you are
Someone fought for you to stay
Whoever you are
Someone fought for you to be

The truth you will become tomorrow
Is a map showing the lineage of how you arrived
Full heart
Full smile
Deep thought
Focused eyes and hands
Set to the beat of brilliance

You are gifted and here
You are proud and you matter
You shatter the doubts
Your bright light shining
Reminiscent of Ali and Garvey and Dangote

And Winfrey and James and Hansberry and we
Have always been brilliant

We have always been worth the time it takes
To learn our names correctly
To love our black and brown and bronze skin tones

We resemble the richest parts
of the earth
Heavy in home
Warm as a stove
Loud like the truth

Wherever you are
Someone fought for you to stay
Whoever you are
Someone fought for you to be
Someone is still fighting for you to be

As fresh and shining as you choose!

ARTIST NOTES

Empowered Reader
by **Vanessa Brantley-Newton**
MEDIUM: Collage on mixed media board
I remember how empowered I felt as a young
girl when I was given a library card. Even
though I am dyslexic, the librarian said to me, "When you
read books they can take you anywhere in the world." I
was inspired by that moment to create this piece. The
young girl wears braids, as they are roads to explore, and
glasses, because she sees clearly where she wants to go. She
has a library card in hand as her passport.

America Doesn't Love Us Back
by **Floyd Cooper**
MEDIUM: Oil erasure and iPad
I was greatly inspired by the words of Doc
Rivers in his response to a reporter's ques-
tion about the shooting of Jacob Blake and murder of

Breonna Taylor: "It's amazing why we keep loving this country, and this country doesn't love us back." August 25, 2020.

Target
by Pat Cummings
MEDIUM: Watercolor, pencil, digital
I wanted to create an image that represented the stark difference between what the Black community sees—what any sentient, sane human would see, actually—and what racists and brutal police, desensitized by racism, see when they encounter a Black person: man, woman, or child. The lyrics of "Lift Every Voice and Sing," a prayer for humanity, provided that fitting contrast to the target icon, which reduces a human being to prey.

This is how I'd sum it up:

Stories told, retold.
Care taken, given.
Lives nurtured, blossoming.
A rhapsody in progress.
Target to the blind.

E Pluribus, II
by Ekua Holmes
MEDIUM: Collage and acrylic on paper
From an ongoing series of collages graphi-

cally exploring community visioning, collaborative planning, and collective action.

Breonna Taylor, Remember Her Name!
by London Ladd
MEDIUM: Mixed media

It was a deeply personal portrait to create.
It wasn't about replicating Breonna Taylor's face but capturing her spirit, who she was beyond the photos. That's why I spent so much time on her eyes, because I wanted the viewer to connect with her. I've done many portraits of well-known people, from Frederick Douglass to MLK, but Taylor's portrait held a greater impact on me because of the climate and circumstances we face as people of color. We have to push forward with knowledge, strength, determination, unity, love, and empathy.

A Black Boy's Journey
by James E. Ransome
MEDIUM: Acrylic and collage

I was at a conference and the keynote speaker was a prominent African American author. He started his speech stating that he was "just as comfortable talking to a group of brothers on a street corner as [he was talking] in the highest halls of academia." His comments made me wonder, are only Black males

149

asked to justify themselves in this way? The image portrays an adolescent boy who has just received a new pair of Jordan sneakers, who will journey outside into those streets. The question is, which will win him over—his family or the streets?

Give Me Flowers
by Shannon Wright
Medium: Mixed media
Give Me Flowers is a call to celebrate the Black lives we have here before they're gone. Situated in a Matryoshka doll–like manner, a Black father, mother, and daughter stand center stage and outwardly proclaim their sadness, their anger, their declaration. Inspired by the works of Aaron Douglas and children's book illustrations, I wanted to play with bold silhouettes that contrast against colorful and organic plant life. The silhouettes of the parents are cloaked in shades of black that serve as a sort of protection to their daughter whose silhouette is a cutaway of a flowery background. She represents new life, life that deserves a chance to grow. And while the parents' shapes are direct contrasts to their child, they are still surrounded by growth and life, life they too deserve to experience in full. *Give Me Flowers* is hope for a future where Black people have a chance to flourish and truly receive their flowers while they're living.

Brother's Murder, Remix
by Eric Velasquez
MEDIUM: Oil on board, digitally remixed

When I was asked to contribute to this anthology, I immediately remembered a painting that I had created over thirty-five years ago. *Brother's Murder* was originally created as an illustration for the *New York Times Magazine* in 1984. I treasure this painting because my young cousin Dennis posed for it when he was coming of age and realizing that life for young African American men was filled with many dangers and fears. Dennis and his older brother, Edgard, along with their friends were really into hip-hop and being DJs back then. My hope was always that being a model for this project ultimately would serve as an inspiration for Dennis and Edgard to move forward and look beyond the limitations of their neighborhood. Today both of my cousins are successful men who have adult children of their own. In light of the Black Lives Matter movement, however, I realized that creating a digitally remixed rendering of my original painting illustrates a powerful truth—my cousins' children still face the same fears and dangers as their fathers. Black. Lives. Matter.

BIOGRAPHIES

 **Henry "Hank" Aaron** (1934–2021) was one of the greatest players to ever play Major League Baseball. During his twenty-three-year career, he broke the career home run record of baseball's icon, Babe Ruth. As Aaron approached the 714 mark that had lasted for more than forty years, he received thousands of hate letters and endured racial remarks and taunts. But they didn't stop him. He broke the record and went on to hit a total of 755 career home runs. Aaron was an activist and a civil rights leader who spoke out against injustice and the unfair treatment of Black Americans. He was inducted into the Baseball Hall of Fame in 1982, where many of his baseball records are listed, and in 2002, President George W. Bush presented him the Presidential Medal of Freedom.

 **James Baldwin** (1924–1987) was an essayist, a playwright, a novelist, and a major voice of the civil rights movement. His first book, *Go Tell It on the Mountain*, was published in 1953. Other works followed,

including *Notes of a Native Son, The Fire Next Time, Giovanni's Room,* and *Another Country,* all of which were popular and received critical acclaim. Considered one of the twentieth century's greatest writers, Baldwin broke new literary ground with the exploration of racial and social issues in his many works. Born in Harlem, New York, Baldwin spent the early part of his writing career in Paris, France. After he returned to the United States, he became a fixture in the civil rights movement, often appearing on television and radio programs sharing his views on race. His novel *If Beale Street Could Talk* was made into a successful movie in 2018. *I Am Not Your Negro,* a 2016 documentary, was based on his unfinished manuscript *Remember This House.*

 **Daisy Gatson Bates** (1914–1999) was an African American civil rights leader and newspaper publisher. She and her journalist husband, Lucius Christopher (L.C.) Bates, operated the *Arkansas State Press,* an African American newspaper in Little Rock. In 1952, Bates became president of the Arkansas chapter of the NAACP and played a crucial role in the fight to end racial segregation in the state. Additionally, her activism and leadership helped allow nine African American students known as "The Little Rock Nine" become the first to attend all-white Central High School in Little Rock. The students first tried to enroll in the school on September 4, 1957,

but a group of angry white people met them with taunts and jeers and some threw objects at them. Despite the enormous animosity they faced, the students were undeterred and remained in school. Bates published her autobiography, *The Long Shadow of Little Rock*, in 1962.

 Born on a farm near Mayesville, South Carolina, **Dr. Mary McLeod Bethune** (1875–1955) rose from humble beginnings to become a world-renowned educator, civil and human rights leader, champion for women and young people, and an advisor to five U.S. presidents. Bethune organized the State Federation of Colored Women's Clubs to fight against segregation and inadequate healthcare for Black children. She founded the first hospital for Black Americans in Daytona Beach, Florida, in addition to founding the National Council of Negro Women. She also helped organize the United Negro College Fund, which raised money to support Black colleges and universities. In 1904, she founded the Daytona Normal and Industrial Institute for Negro Girls in Daytona, Florida. Starting with only five students, Bethune helped grow the school to more than 250 students over the next years. Today, Bethune-Cookman University is a leading HBCU (Historically Black College and University). Honored with many awards and honorary degrees, Bethune's life was celebrated with a memorial statue in Washington, DC, in 1974 and a

postage stamp in 1985. Her final residence is a National Historic Site.

Frederick Douglass (cir. 1818–1895) was born into slavery in Maryland. With the assistance of Anna Murray, a free Black woman, he escaped from that horrible institution when he was a young man. He and Anna married in 1838 and moved to Massachusetts, where Douglass joined the abolitionist movement to end slavery. His dynamic speeches and dedication persuaded others to support the abolitionist cause. An ally of the women's right to vote or suffrage movement and publisher of one of the first Black-owned newspapers, *The North Star*, Douglass wrote three autobiographies, including his most popular, *Narrative of the Life of Frederick Douglass*. By the time of the Civil War, Douglass had become one of the most influential Black men in the country. He conferred with Presidents Abraham Lincoln and Andrew Johnson regarding the treatment of Black Americans and about Black suffrage.

One of the first African American women writers to be published in the United States, **Frances Ellen Watkins Harper** (1825–1911) was a suffragist, teacher, writer, and abolitionist who helped African Americans escaping from slavery on the Underground Railroad. She was in demand as a public speaker and shared the stage with leading abolitionists such as Frederick Douglass. Born free in Baltimore, Maryland, she published her first book of poetry at the age of twenty. Forty-seven years later, she published the widely praised novel *Iola Leroy* (1892). Harper was the first African American woman writer to have a short story published ("The Two Offers," 1859).

CONTRIBUTORS

 **Vanessa Brantley-Newton** is a self-taught illustrator and has attended the Fashion Institute of Technology and the School of Visual Arts in New York. Vanessa believes that all children should see themselves beautifully illustrated in picture books. She is the author and illustrator of *Just Like Me, Grandma's Purse, Don't Let Auntie Mabel Bless the Table,* and *Let Freedom Sing.* She has also illustrated the *New York Times* bestseller *The King of Kindergarten* by Derrick Barnes, *Mary Had a Little Glam* by Tammi Sauer, and *One Love* by Cedella Marley. Vanessa lives in Charlotte, North Carolina, with her husband and daughter and a crazy cat named Stripes. vanessabrantleynewton.com

 **Mahogany L. Browne** is a writer, an organizer, and an educator. She serves as executive director of Bowery Poetry Club, artistic director of Urban Word NYC, and poetry coordinator at St. Francis College. She has received fellowships from the Agnes Gund Foundation, AIR Serenbe, Cave Canem, Poets House, the Andrew W. Mellon Foundation, and the Robert Rauschenberg Foundation.

She is the author of *Chlorine Sky, Woke: A Young Poet's Call to Justice, Woke Baby, Black Girl Magic, Kissing Caskets, #Dear Twitter,* and the upcoming *Vinyl Moon.* She is also the founder of the Woke Baby Book Fair, a nationwide diversity literature campaign, and, as an Art for Justice grantee, is completing her first book of essays on mass incarceration, investigating its impact on women and children. Mahogany lives in Brooklyn. mahoganylbrowne.com

Cofounder of the award-winning blog *The Brown Bookshelf*, **Paula Chase** is a longtime Inclusion Jedi and advocate for diversifying the type of fiction featuring Black characters that's highlighted among educators, librarians, and parents. She's presented and blogged about the need to expand the focus beyond children's literature that centers the pain of the Black experience. Chase is the author of nine children's books. *So Done,* her critically acclaimed middle-grade debut, was named a *Kirkus Reviews* Best Book of the Year. *So Done* and its companions, *Dough Boys* and *Turning Point,* are blazing the trail for books that tackle tough and sometimes taboo topics for younger readers. paulachasebooks.com

 **Lesa Cline-Ransome** has written numerous picture book biographies on notable figures such as Frederick Douglass, Satchel Paige, Claudette Colvin, Pele, and Louis Armstrong, and her books have garnered honors including a Jane Addams Honor, Christopher Award, an NAACP Image Award, *Kirkus Reviews* Best Book, and an NCTE Orbis Pictus Recommended Book. Her verse biography of Harriet Tubman, *Before She Was Harriet,* received a Coretta Scott King Honor for Illustration. Her debut middle-grade novel, *Finding Langston,* received the Scott O'Dell Award for Historical Fiction and the Coretta Scott King Award Author Honor. The companion novels, *Leaving Lymon* and *Being Clem,* complete the Finding Langston trilogy. She lives in the Hudson Valley region of New York with her husband and frequent collaborator, illustrator James Ransome. lesaclineransome.com

 **Floyd Cooper** received a Coretta Scott King Award for his illustrations in *The Blacker the Berry* and Coretta Scott King Honors for *Brown Honey in Broomwheat Tea, Meet Danitra Brown,* and *I Have Heard of a Land.* He is also the recipient of the Virginia Hamilton Literary Award. Born and raised in Tulsa, Oklahoma, Floyd received a degree in fine arts from the University of Oklahoma and, after graduating, worked as an artist for a major greeting

card company. In 1984, he came to New York City to pursue a career as an illustrator of books. Floyd illustrated and/or authored more than 110 children's titles in his celebrated career. He lived in Easton, Pennsylvania, until his passing on July 15, 2021. floydcooper.com

 **Pat Cummings** is the author and/or illustrator of over forty books. Pat teaches children's book courses at Pratt Institute and Parsons and runs a summer Children's Book Boot Camp that brings writers and illustrators together with top editors, art directors, and agents. She serves on the boards of the Authors Guild, the Authors League Fund, and SCBWI and also as chair of the Founders Award Jury for the Society of Illustrators' Original Art Show. Pat's latest books include her debut middle-grade novel, *Trace,* and picture book *Where Is Mommy?* patcummings.com

 **Sharon M. Draper** is a professional educator as well as an accomplished writer of over thirty award-winning books for adolescents and teachers, including *Copper Sun,* winner of the Coretta Scott King Award, the highly acclaimed Jericho and Hazelwood High trilogies, and the *New York Times* bestseller *Out of My Mind.* She served as the National Teacher of the Year, has been honored at the White House six times, and was selected by the U.S. State

Department to be a literary ambassador to the children of Africa as well as China. In 2015, she was honored by the American Library Association as the recipient of the Margaret A. Edwards Award for lifetime literary achievement. Her most recent novel, *Blended*, is also a *New York Times* bestseller. sharondraper.com

Lamar Giles writes for teens and adults across multiple genres, with work appearing on numerous Best Of lists each and every year. He is the author of the acclaimed novels *Fake ID*, *Endangered*, *Overturned*, *Spin*, *The Last Last-Day-of-Summer*, *Not So Pure and Simple*, and *The Last Mirror on the Left* as well as numerous pieces of short fiction. He is a founding member of We Need Diverse Books and resides in Virginia with his wife. lamargiles.com

New York Times bestselling author **Nikki Grimes** is the recipient of the ALAN Award for significant contributions to young adult literature, the Children's Literature Legacy Award for substantial and lasting contributions to literature for children, the Virginia Hamilton Literary Award, and the NCTE Award for Excellence in Poetry for Children. She is the author of the Coretta Scott King Author Award–winner *Bronx Masquerade* and the recipient of five CSK Author Honors. Her most recent titles include the much-honored *Words with Wings, Garvey's Choice, Boston Globe–Horn Book* Honor Book *Between the Lines,* and *One Last Word,* winner of the Lee Bennett Hopkins Poetry Award. Her memoir, *Ordinary Hazards,* won both a Printz Honor and a Sibert Honor. nikkigrimes.com

Ekua Holmes's collage-based illustrations are assembled from cut and torn papers. The colorful layers are infused with the power of hope, faith, and self-determination. For her illustrated work in the children's picture book *Voice of Freedom: Fannie Lou Hamer, Spirit of the Civil Rights Movement,* Holmes received a Caldecott Honor, the Coretta Scott King–John Steptoe New Talent Illustrator Award, a Robert Sibert Honor, and a *Boston Globe–Horn Book* Award. Holmes has also won the coveted Coretta Scott King Illustrator Award for the book *Out of Wonder: Poems Celebrating Poets,* and a second Coretta Scott King Illustrator Award for *The Stuff of Stars.* ekuaholmes.com

Cheryl Willis Hudson is an award-winning children's book author and cofounder with her husband, Wade Hudson, of Just Us Books, Inc., an independent publishing company that focuses on Black-interest books for young people. Her published titles

include the classic *AFRO-BETS ABC Book; Bright Eyes, Brown Skin;* and *Brave. Black. First.: 50+ African American Women Who Changed the World.* She and Wade coedited the middle-grade anthologies *We Rise, We Resist, We Raise Our Voices* and *The Talk: Conversations About Race, Love & Truth.* A member of the PEN America Children's and Young Adult Books Committee, Cheryl has been honored with the Madam C. J. Walker Legacy Award and Children's Book Council Diversity Outstanding Achievement Award. cherylwillishudson.com

 **Curtis Hudson** is a musician/songwriter/ producer who has been playing and composing music since the age of twelve. He began his musical career performing in church and for gospel and R & B groups in Louisiana. During his early twenties, he composed music for three regional plays written by his brother Wade Hudson. As a member of the group "Pure Energy," Curtis composed and produced most of the group's music, including the classic hit song "Holiday" sung by Madonna (co-written by Lisa Stevens), the hit song "Body Work" for the movie *Breakin'* and the mega-hit "Lose Control" by Missy Elliot. Curtis is also the father of the multiplatinum music producer, Eric Hudson.

An author and publisher, **Wade Hudson** is president of Just Us Books, Inc., an independent publisher of books for young people. Among his 30 published books are the middle grade anthologies, *We Rise, We Resist, We Raise Our Voices* and *The Talk: Conversations About Race, Love & Truth*, coedited with his wife, Cheryl; *AFRO-Bets Kids: I'm Going to Be!; Journey*, a poetry collection; and *Defiant*, Wade's memoir of growing up in the Jim Crow South at the height of the civil rights movement. Wade has received the New Jersey Stephen Crane Literary Award, the Ida B. Wells Institutional Leadership Award, the Madam C. J. Walker Legacy Award, and a CBC Diversity Outstanding Achievement Award. wadehudson-authorpublisher.com

Tiffany Jewell is a Black biracial *New York Times* bestselling author, twin sister, first-generation American, cisgender mama, and educator. She is the author of *This Book Is Anti-Racist* and its official companion journal and is currently developing multiple book projects for readers of all ages. She has been working with children and families for over eighteen years and served as a Montessori educator for fifteen. She enjoys exploring social justice with young folks, especially the history of racism and resistance, economic justice, and socially and personally constructed identities. Tiffany continues to work with educators, supporting them in building strong, authentic communities in which every child can be seen and valued. She lives on the homeland of the Pocumtuc and the Nipmuc with her two young storytellers, husband, and a turtle she's had since she was nine years old. anti-biasmontessori.com

 **Keith Knight** is an award-winning cartoonist/writer/illustrator based in North Carolina. His work can be seen in the *Washington Post,* the *New Yorker,* the *Funny Times,* and the *Nib.* He is the illustrator of the Jake the Fake book series and the inspiration and cocreator of the Hulu streaming series *Woke.* kchronicles.com

 **London Ladd** has illustrated numerous critically acclaimed children's books, including *March On!: The Day My Brother Martin Changed the World* and *Frederick's Journey: The Life of Frederick Douglass.* London uses a unique mixed media approach combining cut paper textured with acrylic paint, tissue paper, colored pencil, pen and ink, and digital touches to bring his diverse subjects to life. Each image is steeped in intensity and emotion, a reflection of the artist himself. Varied influences range from classic and contemporary artists to comic

books and graphic novels. "What drives me is discovering new ways of approaching different media and continuing to learn." londonladd.com

Kelly Starling Lyons is an award-winning author whose seventeen titles for children span easy readers, picture books, chapter books, fiction, nonfiction, and series. For more than a decade, Lyons has been creating inspiring books that center around Black heroes; celebrate family, friendship, and heritage; and show all children the storyteller they hold inside. Her titles include *Going Down Home with Daddy*, *Sing a Song: How "Lift Every Voice and Sing" Inspired Generations*, *Dream Builder: The Story of Architect Philip Freelon*, *Tiara's Hat Parade*, and the Jada Jones chapter book series. Her easy reader series with illustrator Nina Mata, Ty's Travels, has received starred reviews, and *Ty's Travels Zip, Zoom!* was a Geisel Honor Book. kellystarlinglyons.com

Kwame Mbalia is a husband, father, writer, *New York Times* bestselling author, and former pharmaceutical metrologist, in that order. His debut middle-grade novel, *Tristan Strong Punches a Hole in the Sky*, received a Coretta Scott King Author Honor Award. A Howard University graduate and a Midwesterner now living in

North Carolina, he enjoys impromptu dance sessions and Cheez-Its. kwamembalia.com

 **DeRay Mckesson** is a civil rights activist focused primarily on issues of innovation, equity, and justice. Born and raised in Baltimore, he graduated from Bowdoin College and holds honorary doctorates from The New School and the Maryland Institute College of Art. DeRay has advocated for issues related to children, youth, and families since he was a teen. As a leading voice in the Black Lives Matter movement and a cofounder of Campaign Zero, DeRay has worked to connect individuals with knowledge and tools, and provide citizens and policy makers with commonsense policies that ensure equity. He has been praised by President Obama for his work as a community organizer, has advised officials at all levels of government and internationally, and continues to provide capacity to activists, organizers, and influencers to make an impact. deray.com

 **Robert H. Miller** has written award-winning children's books about the role of African Americans in settling the Old West. The four-book series Reflections of a Black Cowboy, includes *Cowboys*, *Buffalo Soldiers*, *Pioneers*, and *Mountain Men*. He is also the author of the

picture-book series Stories from the Forgotten West and the chapter book *A Pony for Jeremiah* as well as a playwright and a writer for film and television. Robert is an adjunct professor at Temple University in Philadelphia and at Rider University in New Jersey.

Denene Millner is the *New York Times* bestselling author of thirty-one books, including *The Fresh Princess*, inspired by Will Smith's *The Fresh Prince of Bel-Air*, and *The Vow*, the novel on which the Lifetime movie *With This Ring* was based. Denene is the editor of Denene Millner Books, a Simon & Schuster imprint that won Newbery and Caldecott honors and the *Kirkus* Prize for Children's Literature in its debut year. Denene also cohosts Georgia Public Broadcasting's *A Seat at the Table*, a talk show about Black women, and hosts *Speakeasy with Denene*, a podcast that examines Blackness. @MyBrownBaby

Jerdine Nolen is the beloved author of many award-winning books, including *Big Jabe; Thunder Rose*, a Coretta Scott King Illustrator Honor Book; and *Hewitt Anderson's Great Big Life*, a Bank Street Best Book of the Year—all illustrated by Kadir Nelson. She is also the author of *Eliza's Freedom Road*, which was an ALA-YALSA Best Fiction for Young Adults nominee; *Raising Dragons*, which received a Christopher Award; and *Harvey Potter's Balloon Farm*, which won the Kentucky Bluegrass Award. Her other books include *Plantzilla*, which was a Book Sense 76 Selection; *Irene's Wish*, which *Kirkus Reviews* called "delightful and memorable" in a starred review; and *Calico Girl*, which was a *Kirkus Reviews* Best Book of the Year. Her recent picture book, *Freedom Bird: A Tale of Hope and Courage*, received a *Kirkus* starred review and was a Parents' Choice Silver Award recipient. jerdinenolen.com

Adedayo Perkovich is a senior member of the Young People's Chorus of New York City, and oboe student and soprano section leader in the Juilliard Music Advancement Program. She is a reporter and youth mentor for the *IndyKids* national youth newspaper, and was a kid reporter for Scholastic Kid Press Corps, where she interviewed director Ava DuVernay and First Lady Michelle Obama. In her spare time she writes poetry, paints inspirational quotes, takes walks, and talks with her cat.

James E. Ransome has illustrated over seventy books for children. His newest book, *The Bell Rang*, which he wrote and illustrated, has received four starred reviews and was a *Kirkus* Best Book. His books have garnered numerous accolades, including Coretta Scott

King Awards, a *Boston Globe-Horn Book* Honor, ALA Notables, a Jane Addams Award, and NAACP Image Awards. He has created murals for Poughkeepsie's Adriance Memorial Library, the Children's Museum of Indianapolis, and the National Underground Railroad Freedom Center in Cincinnati. James received his BFA from Pratt Institute and lives in Rhinebeck, New York, with his wife and frequent collaborator, author Lesa Cline-Ransome. jamesransome.com

Ronald L. Smith is an award-winning writer of children's literature, including the middle-grade novels *Black Panther: The Young Prince*, *The Mesmerist*, *The Owls Have Come to Take Us Away*, and *Gloom Town*, a Junior Library Guild Selection. His first novel, *Hoodoo*, earned him the 2016 Coretta Scott King–John Steptoe New Talent Author Award and the ILA Award for Intermediate Fiction from the International Literacy Association. Before he became a full-time writer, he worked in advertising and wrote TV commercials for big corporations. He is much happier writing books for young people. strangeblackflowers.com

Nic Stone is the author of the #1 *New York Times* bestseller and William C. Morris Award finalist *Dear Martin*, its *New York Times* bestselling sequel *Dear Justyce*, and the middle-grade *New York Times* bestseller

Clean Getaway. The Atlanta native and Spelman College graduate is also the author of the acclaimed novels *Odd One Out* and *Jackpot* for teens, *Shuri: A Black Panther Novel,* and *Fast Pitch,* a middle-grade novel that couples Nic's love of softball and the movie *The Sandlot* with her desire to see more Black female athletes represented. Nic lives in Atlanta with her adorable little family. nicstone.info

 **Don Tate** is an award-winning illustrator of books for children, including *Swish!: The Slam-Dunking, Alley-Ooping, High-Flying Harlem Globetrotters; Carter Reads the Newspaper; No Small Potatoes: Junius G. Groves and His Kingdom in Kansas; Whoosh!: Lonnie Johnson's Super-Soaking Stream of Inventions;* and is a contributor to the anthology *The Talk: Conversations About Race, Love & Truth.* He is also the writer and illustrator of *Pigskins to Paintbrushes: The Story of Football-Playing Artist Ernie Barnes* and *William Still and His Freedom Stories: The Father of the Underground Railroad,* and authored the Ezra Jack Keats Award winners *Poet: The Remarkable Story of George Moses Horton* and *It Jes' Happened: When Bill Traylor Started to Draw.* Don is a founding host of *The Brown Bookshelf,* a blog dedicated to promoting books created by African American authors and illustrators and a member of We Need Diverse Books, an organization created by children's book lovers who advocate for essential changes in the publishing industry to

produce and promote literature that reflects and honors the lives of all young people. He lives in Austin, Texas, with his family. dontate.com

Eric Velasquez earned his BFA from the School of Visual Arts and has illustrated over thirty children's books. His first picture book, *The Piano Man* by Debbi Chocolate, won the Coretta Scott King–John Steptoe Award for New Talent, and in 2010 Eric was awarded an NAACP Image Award for his work in *Our Children Can Soar*, which he collaborated on with twelve notable children's book illustrators. Eric also wrote and illustrated *Grandma's Records* and its follow-up *Grandma's Gift*, which won a Pura Belpré Award for illustration, and *Octopus Stew*, which has gathered rave reviews. Eric's illustrated *Schomburg: The Man Who Built a Library* by Carole Boston Weatherford earned five starred reviews and won a Walter Award from the We Need Diverse Books organization as well as the SCBWI's Golden Kite Award. His picture book, *Ruth Objects: The Life of Ruth Bader Ginsburg,* honors the legacy of the late Supreme Court justice. Eric's latest book *She Was the First! The Trailblazing Life of Shirley Chisholm* was awarded the 2021 NAACP Image Award for outstanding literature for children. Eric teaches book illustration at the Fashion Institute of Technology in New York. ericvelasquez.com

 **Carole Boston Weatherford** has written over fifty books, including the Caldecott Honor winners: *Freedom in Congo Square; Moses: When Harriet Tubman Led Her People to Freedom;* and *Voice of Freedom: Fannie Lou Hamer, Spirit of the Civil Rights Movement,* which was also a Robert F. Sibert Honor Book. In addition, she is the author of *Unspeakable: The Tulsa Race Massacre* and the recent releases *BOX: Henry Brown Mails Himself to Freedom; By and By: Charles Albert Tindley, the Father of Gospel Music; R-E-S-P-E-C-T: Aretha Franklin, the Queen of Soul;* and *The Roots of Rap: 16 Bars on the 4 Pillars of Hip-Hop.* A recipient of the North Carolina Award for Literature, Carole has been inducted to the North Carolina Literary Hall of Fame. Baltimore born, she is a professor at Fayetteville State University. cbweatherford.com

 **Alicia D. Williams** is the author of *Jump at the Sun: The True Life Tale of Unstoppable Storycatcher Zora Neale Hurston* and *Genesis Begins Again,* which received Newbery and *Kirkus* Prize honors, was a William C. Morris Award finalist, and won the Coretta Scott King–John Steptoe Award for New Talent. Alicia is a graduate of the MFA program at Hamline University, is an oral storyteller in the African American tradition, and resides in Charlotte, North Carolina. aliciadwilliams.com

Shannon Wright is an illustrator and cartoonist based out of Richmond, Virginia. She has illustrated two picture books, *My Mommy Medicine* by Edwidge Danticat and *I'm Gonna Push Through!* by Jasmyn Wright, along with her debut graphic novel, *Twins* by Varian Johnson. She likes capturing joyous moments and making personal and original stories invoking nostalgia rooted from her own childhood and life around her. Shannon graduated with a BFA from Virginia Commonwealth University, where she coteaches a comics course during the summer. shannon-wright.com

Ibi Zoboi was born in Port-au-Prince, Haiti, and holds an MFA in writing for children and young adults from Vermont College of Fine Arts. Her YA novel *American Street* was a National Book Award finalist, and her debut middle-grade novel, *My Life as an Ice Cream Sandwich*, was a *New York Times* bestseller. She is the author of *Pride*, a contemporary YA remix of Jane Austen's *Pride and Prejudice*, and editor of the anthology *Black Enough: Stories of Being Young & Black in America*. Her most recent bestseller, *Punching the Air*, is a YA novel in verse, coauthored by prison reform activist Yusef Salaam of the Exonerated Five. Raised in New York City, Ibi now lives in New Jersey with her husband and their three children. ibizoboi.net

ABOUT THE BLACK LIVES MATTER MOVEMENT

The #BlackLivesMatter movement was begun in 2013 by Patrisse Cullors, Alicia Garza, and Opal Tometi. It was in response to the acquittal of George Zimmerman, who, in 2012, shot and killed unarmed, seventeen-year-old Trayvon Martin. The movement gained momentum and support both nationally and internationally as it addressed the continuing killing of unarmed Black men and women across the country. The recent movement continues a long tradition of Black Americans struggling to ensure that Black lives are recognized and respected and that Black people receive the same fair treatment and real justice as all other Americans. Halting the wanton taking of Black life is also about recognizing those microaggressions, abuses, oversights, and discriminatory acts that Black people face daily. It is about the myriad ways that Black people have made a way for themselves despite living in a hostile environment. How they have determined to stay whole when too often they are considered less than.

SOURCES

"James Baldwin's Great Debate" by Wade Hudson
Baldwin, James, and William F. Buckley. "The
  legendary debate that laid down US political lines
  on race, justice and history." "Has the American
  Dream been achieved at the expense of the
  American Negro?" debate. Filmed February 18,
  1965, Cambridge, UK. Audio restoration by Adam
  D'Arpino, August 8, 2019. Video of debate, 58:42.
  aeon.co/videos/the-legendary-debate-that-laid-
  down-us-political-lines-on-race-justice-and-history

"Baldwin-Buckley race debate still resonates 55
  years on." Produced by Zachary Green. *PBS News
  Hour*, February 16, 2020. Video, 9:00. pbs.org/
  newshour/show/baldwin-buckley-race-debate-still-
  resonates-55-years-on

Regas, Rima. "Transcript: James Baldwin Debates
  William F. Buckley (1965)." *Blog #42*, June 7,
  2015. Transcript of speech delivered at Cambridge

University, February 18, 1965. rimaregas.
com/2015/06/07/transcript-james-baldwin-debates-
william-f-buckley-1965-blog42/

"Hank Aaron Passes on the Legacy" by Wade Hudson
Aaron, Hank. "When Baseball Mattered." *New York
Times*, April 13, 1997. nytimes.com/1997/04/13/
opinion/when-baseball-mattered.html

"The Slave Mother" by Frances Ellen Watkins Harper
Harper, Frances Ellen Watkins. "The Slave Mother."
In *African American Poetry: 250 Years of Struggle
& Song*, 59. Edited by Kevin Young. New York:
Library of America, 2020.

**"Excerpt from What to the Slave Is the Fourth of July?"
by Frederick Douglass**
Douglass, Frederick. *The Life and Writings of
Frederick Douglass* Vol. 2, *Pre–Civil War Decade
1850–1860*, 181–189, edited by Philip S. Foner.
New York: International Publishers Co., Inc.,
1950.

**"Letter from Daisy Bates to Roy Wilkins: The
Treatment of the Little Rock Nine"**
Bates, Daisy. Daisy Bates to NAACP Executive
Secretary Roy Wilkins on the treatment of the

Little Rock Nine, December 17, 1957. Typed
letter. NAACP Records, Manuscript Division,
Library of Congress. loc.gov/exhibits/naacp/the
-civil-rights-era.html

**"Dr. Mary McLeod Bethune's 'Last Will and
Testament'" by Cheryl Willis Hudson and Wade
Hudson**
Bethune, Dr. Mary McLeod. "Dr. Bethune's Last
Will & Testament." Bethune-Cookman University.
Accessed March 1, 2021. cookman.edu/about_bcu/
history/lastwill_testament.html

PHOTO CREDITS

p. 9 and p. 153: James Baldwin photograph by Anfeo Sjak-kelien Vollebregt accessed via Wikimedia Commons; p. 21 and p. 153: Henry "Hank" Aaron photograph by LBJ Presidential Library accessed via Wikimedia Commons at commons.wikimedia.org/wiki/File:Hank_Aaron_13704 _5948.jpg; p. 43 and p. 158: Frances Ellen Watkins Harper photograph via the WCTU Archives, Evanston, IL; p. 59 and p. 156: Frederick Douglass photograph by Frank W. Legg via the National Archives; p. 79 and p. 154: Daisy Gatson Bates photograph by Getty Images; p. 86: phone art created by Trish Parcell; p. 109 and p. 155: Dr. Mary McLeod Bethune photograph by Carl Van Vechten via the Library of Congress; p. 159: Vanessa Brantley-Newton photograph by Zoe S. Newton; Mahogany L. Browne photograph by Jennie Bergvist; p. 160: Paula Chase photograph by Capture the Seen Photos; p. 161: Lesa Cline-Ransome photograph by John Halpern; Floyd Cooper photograph courtesy of artist; p. 162: Pat Cummings photograph by Marvin Lee; Sharon M. Draper photograph courtesy of author; p. 163: Lamar Giles photograph by Adrienne Giles; Nikki Grimes photograph by Aaron Lemen; p. 164: Ekua Holmes photograph by Song KaiEsi Holmes; Cheryl Willis Hudson photograph by Stephan Hudson; p. 165: Curtis Hudson photograph by Stephan Hudson; p. 166: Wade Hudson photograph by Stephan Hudson; Tiffany Jewell photograph courtesy of author; p. 167: Keith Knight photograph by *Durham Magazine*; London Ladd photograph by Roger DeNuth; p. 168: Kelly Starling Lyons photograph by Lundie's Photography; Kwame Mbalia photograph courtesy of author; p. 169: DeRay Mckesson photograph by Campaign Zero; Robert H. Miller photograph courtesy of author; p. 170: Denene Millner photograph by Lila Chiles; Jerdine Nolen photograph by Houghton Mifflin Harcourt; p. 171: Adedayo Perkovich photograph by Kennady Cox; James E. Ransome photograph by James E. Ransome; p. 172: Ronald L. Smith photograph by Erik Kvalsvik; Nic Stone photograph by Nigel Livingstone; p. 173: Don Tate photograph by Sam Bond; p. 174: Eric Velasquez photograph courtesy of artist; p. 175: Carole Boston Weatherford photograph by Gerald Young; Alicia D. Williams photograph by Jasiatic Photography; p. 176: Shannon Wright photograph by Sarah Schultz Taylor; Ibi Zoboi photograph by Richard Louissant

CONTRIBUTOR COPYRIGHT

Empowered Reader by Vanessa Brantley-Newton copyright © 2021
by Vanessa Brantley-Newton

"Your Breath Is a Song" by Mahogany L. Browne copyright © 2021
by Mahogany L. Browne

"Black Butterfly" by Paula Chase copyright © 2021 by Paula Chase

"At Our Kitchen Table" by Lesa Cline-Ransome copyright © 2021
by Lesa Cline-Ransome

America Doesn't Love Us Back by Floyd Cooper copyright © 2021 by Floyd Cooper

Target by Pat Cummings copyright © 2021 by Pat Cummings

"Miracle Child" by Sharon M. Draper copyright © 2021 by Sharon M. Draper

"The Storms and Sunshine of My Life" by Lamar Giles copyright © 2021 by Lamar Giles

"Witness" by Nikki Grimes copyright © 2021 by Nikki Grimes

E Pluribus, II by Ekua Holmes copyright © 2021 by Ekua Holmes

"Recognize!" by Cheryl Willis Hudson copyright © 2021 by Cheryl Willis Hudson

"Mary McLeod Bethune's 'Last Will and Testament'" by Cheryl Willis Hudson and Wade
Hudson copyright © 2021 by Cheryl Willis Hudson and Wade Hudson

"Freedom in the Music" by Curtis Hudson copyright © 2021 by Curtis Hudson

"Black Lives Have Always Mattered" by Wade Hudson © 2021 by Wade Hudson

"Hank Aaron Passes on the Legacy" by Wade Hudson copyright © 2021 by Wade Hudson

"James Baldwin's Great Debate" by Wade Hudson copyright © 2021 by Wade Hudson

"Foreword" by Wade Hudson and Cheryl Willis Hudson copyright © 2021
by Wade Hudson and Cheryl Willis Hudson

"Back to Myself" by Tiffany Jewell copyright © 2021 by Tiffany Jewell

"Famous Blerds in History" by Keith Knight copyright © 2021 by Keith Knight

Breonna Taylor, Remember Her Name! by London Ladd copyright © 2021 by London Ladd

"Joy Lives in You" by Kelly Starling Lyons copyright © 2021 by Kelly Starling Lyons

"Self-Reflection" by Kwame Mbalia copyright © 2021 by Kwame Mbalia

"An Interview with DeRay Mckesson" questions copyright © 2021
by Wade Hudson and Cheryl Willis Hudson

"An Interview with DeRay Mckesson" responses copyright © 2021 by DeRay Mckesson

185